What the critics are saying…

4.5 hearts! …love scenes are very hot and hold nothing back … ~ *Angel Brewer, The Romance Studio*

4 hearts! …exciting…YUM!! More, more, more!!! ~ *Thia McClain, The Romance Reader's Connection*

"…wonderful, sexy, and amazing …A HERO'S KISS ratchets up the intensity and keeps it at fever pitch throughout the entire story" ~ *Angela Camp, Romance Reviews Today*

4 stars! …has something for everyone - erotic sex, betrayal, suspenseful action, and passionate love. If you like your books with explicit hot sex and a touch of suspense, this one is for you. It is quite a delight to read and enjoy…" ~ *Elise Lynne, CataRomance Reviews*

5 angels!…love scenes were extremely hot and well written, the storyline was fabulous, the characters were amazingly well rounded, and the ending was perfect …" ~ *Serena, Fallen Angel Reviews*

5 cups "…exciting…a sensual story full of sexual release…!" ~ *Sheryl, Coffee Time Romance*

A Hero's Kiss
Jan Springer

ELLORA'S CAVE
ROMANTICA PUBLISHING

An Ellora's Cave Romantica Publication

www.ellorascave.com

Heroes at Heart: A Hero's Kiss

ISBN # 1419952218
ALL RIGHTS RESERVED.
A Hero's Kiss Copyright© 2005 Jan Springer
Edited by: Mary Moran
Cover art by: Syneca

Electronic book Publication: January, 2005
Trade paperback Publication: July, 2005

Excerpt from *A Hero Betrayed* Copyright © Jan Springer 2004
Excerpt from *A Hero's Welcome* Copyright © Jan Springer 2003

Warning:

Also by Jan Springer:

Heroes at Heart 1: A Hero's Welcome
Heroes at Heart 2: A Hero Escapes
Heroes at Heart 3: A Hero Betrayed
Holiday Heat anthology
Outlaw Lovers: Jude Outlaw
Outlaw Lovers: The Claiming

A Hero's Kiss

Heroes at Heart

Chapter One
On the planet of Paradise…

Drifting upwards through the thick layers of sleep, United States astronaut and kindergarten teacher Piper Hero became very aware of a pair of wonderfully strong hands clasping her hips, preventing her from grinding herself into the erotic pleasure pulsing through her vagina as a rough tongue swiped against her throbbing clitoris.

She opened her eyes and stared in stunned fascination at the stranger's head buried between her writhing legs, her very naked legs that were curled over each of his massive muscular shoulders.

Oh, my goodness!

Was this a fantasy sex dream?

Or was it reality?

Hot sensual lips nibbled at her slick labia, and she gasped with pleasure as sharp teeth bit gently into her tender flesh.

It felt so good.

So unbelievably good.

A burst of heat sliced up her vagina as his thick tongue invaded her drenched channel.

Piper closed her eyes against the sweet agony.

Oh, yes! Please!

Fuck me with your tongue! Do it!

Her legs tensed, her cunt trembled with want.

She dug her fingernails into the mattress beneath her.

Her breathing grew labored. Perspiration dashed across her fevered skin but it did nothing to extinguish the powerful fire lunging through her veins.

In and out of her quivering pussy, his tongue plunged as if it was a miniature cock, her vaginal muscles grabbing at the thick intruder trying to suction him deeper inside.

The climax drew closer.

She tried to gather her thoughts. Tried to figure out whom this stranger might be but she needed to come so badly.

Weakly she reached out, her fingers sifting through his silky black hair as she grabbed the back of his head, pulling his sweet mouth deeper into her pussy.

Her legs moved off his shoulders and tightened around his neck.

She squeezed hard.

Real hard.

Rough beard stubble raked erotically against her sensitive inner thighs making her spin quickly toward her orgasm. The intense way his fingers dug into her fleshy hips made her realize he wasn't a dream.

He was real!

She really was naked in a strange room with a man tongue fucking her, her body yearning for release.

Despite her sudden understanding of the situation, she could do nothing but give in to the tormenting need building inside her pussy.

She ground her pulsing pussy harder into his face, the sweet agony of his mouth sucking the cream from her body making her shudder.

Making her cry out.

He continued thrusting his tongue into her tiny slit, stretching her small opening with each powerful plunge.

Hot lust consumed her.

Convulsions raged through her, and she twisted her hips against his powerful hands.

The sexual tension burst, intense pleasure spreading outward like an explosion.

Her thoughts splintered.

A sexual inferno took hold of her senses.

Powerful spasms slammed into her one after another until she was crying out.

His hot tongue continued to fuck her.

The delicious torment was endless.

Thrashing her head back and forth on the pillow, she rode the brilliant waves as he continued to suck her sexual cream from her body.

When the climax ebbed, she lay gasping for air, her arms falling limply from his head to her sides, her entire body covered in a blissfully cool perspiration.

She felt dazed as his hot tongue slipped from her quivering vagina and his face moved away. Uncurling her trembling legs from around his hot neck, he gently placed them upon the mattress.

"You eating her again?" came an amused chuckle from somewhere to her right.

Piper's blood ran cold as she realized another man was in the room.

"She came out of the fever sex dream for a few moments. Then her climax hit and she must have gone under again." The man who'd just tongue fucked her sounded deep and dark, unleashing another shiver of lust through her veins.

Who were these two men? Where was she? Why had this stranger just given her the best orgasm of her life?

She tried to ignore the wonderful sparks grazing the inside of her thighs as a pair of tender hands used a warm, damp cloth to intimately wipe away her lust-induced stickiness.

She was too weak to be ashamed at being splayed out naked in front of two strangers. Too weary to stop him from touching her, not that she wanted him to stop, his hands were being so gentle with her, she couldn't believe any man could be so caring.

"Perhaps you should let me try fucking her with my cock, Jarod?" came his companion's eager reply. "I've been known to fuck women out of sex fevers before."

Sex fevers? What in the world was that?

A cool palm splayed over her warm forehead.

"Fever is almost gone. But she is too weak for a proper fucking, Taylor."

Piper let out a slow breath of relief wondering what in the world was going on here. Where was she? What had happened?

"You are right," Taylor chuckled heartily. "But I can hope, can I not? By the way, how does she taste?"

12

There was a brief silence. To her shock, she realized she craved to hear his answer.

"Sweeter than the sweetest fruit," came Jarod's husky whisper.

Oh, my gosh! The man was a poet. Not.

She wanted to open her eyes and study the face of Jarod, the man who had brought her such intense pleasure, but while he'd been seducing her clitoris and bringing on that mind-blowing orgasm, she'd been too busy with her pleasure to check out his features.

She didn't dare open her eyes now and let them know she was awake.

At least not until she could gather her chaotic thoughts and think straight.

"I've almost got dinner cooked. You coming down?" Taylor asked.

He was further away now.

"Be there in a minute."

The intimate wiping of her body stopped, and she waited anxiously for them to leave.

The set of footsteps further away slowly faded as one of them left but the other man, the one named Jarod, was staying behind.

She could hear *him*.

His breath sounded rapid and shallow. As if he was aroused. As if he wanted to take her again.

Maybe this time with his cock!

If his cock was half as good as his tongue…

Piper shivered inwardly at that delicious thought.

And she could literally *feel* him watching her.

Could *feel* his scorching stare drift over her small, pert breasts.

Her nipples trembled in anticipation, and she ached to have his mouth feast upon her flesh. To have his hot kisses graze across her slightly rounded abdomen and dive between her legs.

Her tender clit swelled eagerly yet again.

Moistness accumulated inside her channel readying herself for his penetration.

She clenched her teeth as pleasant sensations rippled through her pussy at the thought of being fucked senseless.

And he wasn't even touching her!

Was he waiting for her to awaken? So he could mouth fuck her again? Not that she didn't want him to…

Piper inhaled sharply at the way her thoughts were heading toward sex again.

What in the world was wrong with her? She'd never been sexually attracted so blindly to a stranger before. Could it have to do with the orgasm he'd just given her? Could it be because she'd been without a man for so long that it had affected her body?

"You're awake."

It was the voice of Jarod.

Goodness! What should she do?

"Open your eyes, woman. Open them," he coaxed softly.

He was very near to her now.

She could feel the heat from him slam into her exposed skin. His mouth hovered so close that his warm breath fondled her earlobe causing it to tingle erotically.

She savored his clean masculine scent. Loved the way his gentle fingertips touched her chin. She couldn't stop herself from opening her eyes.

The instant she saw him something wonderful slammed into her chest.

Dangerous warrior was her first thought. Sexy as sin was her second.

His hair shone a midnight black. Parted in the middle it fell down to his shoulders like a dark waterfall. He had a sun-darkened face with strong angles, his nose seemed slightly off-center as if it had been broken and hadn't healed properly.

Hot blood heated her when she noted the sexy, black pirate patch covering his right eye. The patch did little to hide the jagged scar that ran out from under it. Curving in a half-moon, the raised skin climbed over the top of his flushed cheekbone and ended beneath his earlobe.

The scar gave him a threatening appearance but it was a direct contrast to the warm way his one eye looked at her.

Piper's gaze drifted to his sensually shaped mouth. She remembered how her thighs had trembled with lust as his soft lips eagerly suckled her pussy.

Sweet heavens! Get a grip, woman!

This was no time to be sexually aware of a strange man who'd just orally fucked her without her permission.

"How do you feel?" he asked. A tanned finger eased up along her jaw line to tenderly caress her cheek.

His touch sent odd little tingles through her flesh. What in the world could she say, other than please tongue fuck me again?

From this vantage point, she could tell he was sitting on the floor right beside her. It gave her an up close and personal look at the thick welts and healed scars lashed across his broad, naked chest and wonderfully wide shoulders.

Whip marks.

She bit her bottom lip.

What had happened to him? And what in the world had happened to her?

"W-where am I?"

"You're in The Outer Limits," came his soft reply.

"The Outer Limits?"

He cocked his head slightly to one side with curiosity. Gosh, he looked so cute when he did that.

"What…happened to me?"

"I was hoping you could tell me. We found you in the Fever Swamps near the Acid Zone while we were out hunting."

Piper frowned. The Outer Limits? The Acid Zone? Fever Swamps? What was with these weird names?

"You drank too much of the swamp water. I've done my best to suck out the poisons. Now that you are awake you should be fine now."

Suck out the… What was he saying?

"Poisons?" she whispered.

His forehead furrowed in puzzlement.

"You've had fever sex dreams from the brown water for days."

"Fever sex dreams?" Was this guy serious?

"If I hadn't made you orgasm constantly, you would have died."

No way. This guy was kidding her—looking for an excuse to have his head between her legs.

Without warning, visions and feelings swept over her.

There was darkness, the silhouette of a man somewhere nearby, watching her. The need to be sexually penetrated, the pulsing agony of wanting to climax but not being able to. Her desperate cries, her agonizing screams as she'd begged to be fucked.

Oh, my gosh! He wasn't kidding.

She remembered the brown water. It had tasted awful as she'd frantically fought against the weeds that seemed to act like strong fingers curling around her ankles trying to drag her under.

Oh, God!

Her sisters! Kayla and Kinley!

Where were they?

Piper struggled to get up. But the weakness claiming her and the stranger placing a strong hand across her naked chest prevented her from moving.

This time there was no sexual reaction to his touch on her part. There was only fear and confusion twisting through her brain. And an odd soreness in her ribs not to mention in other areas of her body as a result of the crash.

"Stay still and rest. You cannot go anywhere yet."

"My sisters, where are they?"

He frowned. "There are others?"

"Yes! Two others. Please…tell me they're okay."

She could literally feel the bitter bile of anxiety for their safety mount against her sanity. And she could feel an odd weakness swooping in for the kill.

"There was no sign of anyone else."

Her heart clenched painfully at the dreaded words. Hot tears bubbled into her eyes and streamed a burning trail down her cheeks.

Tender masculine fingers gently brushed them away. "We found only you. Just the way you are. Naked and feverish."

Naked. There hadn't been time to dress.

It had happened so quickly.

The alarm had shrieked through the spaceship, ripping them out of their sleep pods, thrusting them into the smoky cabin. There hadn't been any time to do anything except yell directions at each other in a desperate effort to try and find out what had gone wrong, and pray they'd be able to fix it before they hit the planet or, at the very least, pray they would die a quick death upon impact.

Maybe her sisters' prayers had been answered?

Maybe they were dead?

A sob caught in her throat. For a moment, she thought she might be sick, but she quickly gathered her shattered emotions as she realized one shred of hope remained.

The last time she'd seen her sisters, they were alive. They'd been bruised and battered, but they'd all gotten out of the wreck.

And they'd swum with her through the endless, brown-water swamp. One on each side of her, making sure they stayed together, making sure she kept her head above water while exhaustion and pain had tugged at her.

She remembered reaching the shore and collapsing only to wake up here with this man's head between her legs.

Piper inhaled a deep, steady breath.

Okay. Her sisters had survived the crash.

So where were they? Why had they left her alone?

"What is your name?" he asked.

"Piper," she whispered.

"These others. Are they in the same danger you were in?"

"Yes, we…" she hesitated, not quite sure what to reveal to him. She remembered the message her three brothers had sent back with their spaceship when it had returned to Earth without them over two years ago.

They'd said women ruled this planet. They'd said men weren't allowed to be educated. They weren't even supposed to speak unless spoken to and were considered nothing more than slaves.

That's why the three of them, her and her sisters had decided to come here to search for their brothers and take them back home away from this insanity.

Yet, this man was talking. He seemed normal enough. Except for him tongue-fucking her…

Okay, so maybe this type of behavior was normal for men around here. Maybe not.

This just wasn't the time to pussyfoot around. She needed to tell this guy the truth.

"We're…looking for the Hero brothers. Joe, Ben and Buck," she explained.

At her words, there was the slightest tightening of his sensually shaped lips. Other than that, there was no sign he knew who she was talking about.

Desperation clawed at her insides. The weakness claiming her body grew stronger. She had to get answers before she caved in and blacked out.

"Do…you know them?" She blinked away the black waves hovering in front of her eyes. "Have you any idea…where they are?"

He shook his head.

The gentle caressing of his fingers against her jaw stopped. The warmth in his blue eye slowly vanished and turned to ice.

Piper shivered.

His lips tightened into a thin line.

"Rest. You are very weak. I will brew a broth for you."

He was right. She was so weak she could barely think straight. Could barely sense the odd change in his demeanor.

Her eyes fluttered sleepily. She forced them to stay open. She needed to stay awake.

Needed to focus. Needed to find them.

"What about my…sisters?" she whispered. "Please…go and look for them."

"I will go. Do not worry."

Relief spilled through her, and this time she couldn't stop her eyes from fluttering closed.

"Thank you. Thank…you so much," she whispered.

Blackness swooped in around her and Piper slept.

* * * * *

"Where are you going?" Jarod asked a few minutes later when he found his friend stuffing food into one of their tattered knapsacks.

Taylor looked up at him, his warm brown eyes filled with excitement. "I was listening at the doorway. Heard what she said about the other females. I'm going to look for them."

Uneasiness slithered through him. The last thing they needed was to take any chances with the words of this woman. She could be lying.

"It is not safe. You should not go."

"But you said you would go. Instead, I'll take your place."

"I only agreed because she was upset. She cannot heal if she is upset. Besides you very well know this woman could have been sent into The Outer Limits on a mission to destroy those talking Hero males or to recapture us."

"I don't think she is one of them. I have been forced to fuck every woman in every hub for miles around. I have not seen this one before. Have you?"

"No, but it's not a chance I'm willing to take. She could have been recruited from somewhere else."

Taylor frowned. "You would sacrifice two possible innocents because you don't trust women?"

Without hesitation, Jarod nodded.

"I know you've sworn off women, but I haven't," Taylor said softly.

"Fine! If you're so desperate for a fuck, then use the one we have here," Jarod growled.

To his utter shock, he realized if Taylor so much as took him up on his offer or touched a hair on her head, he would kill him.

As if reading his thoughts, Taylor smiled.

"Deny it all you want but I saw the way you cared for her when she was ill. I saw the tenderness in your hands as you washed the fever sweat from her aroused body. I watched the frantic way you devoured her pussy while she was trapped in her sex dreams in hopes she would open her pretty green eyes."

Taylor hoisted the knapsack onto his back. "Admit it. You like her and she is petite, just the way you like them. If I remember correctly, you always preferred to fuck the petite women in the hubs. Said their channels were tighter than all the others and your orgasms were more powerful. And now that you have had your first taste of a woman in over two years, you will not be able to stop yourself from taking this one... Even though you say you hate women for enslaving us...perhaps you can avenge your lusts on this one, my friend? Perhaps then you will be in a better mood, and not bite my head off every time dinner is not to your taste?"

"You are a bad cook. And I told you, I do not want her," Jarod lied.

Anger seethed inside him at the thought he wanted this woman. Maybe wanted was the wrong word. Craved. That was the proper word.

He craved to touch her heart-shaped face, run his fingers over her silky cheeks, taste her succulent lips and to tangle his fingers into those soft, brown tresses that draped down to the middle of her back, and he craved to pry apart her pussy lips once again and plunge his tongue into her and drink her sweet sex cream from her body.

Jarod licked his lips, remembering that she'd tasted sweeter than any other woman he'd been forced to service.

He frowned and chastised himself. It was only his training speaking to him. Since he'd been a youngster, he'd been trained to please women. He'd had many of them. And he'd never craved them like he now desired this delicious female.

Lust and sex were a hard habit to break.

As if trying to prove to himself that this woman named Piper meant nothing to him, he said, "I told you, she's all yours to do with what you wish."

"And I told you if she was all mine, you would have allowed me to fuck her by now. She would have awoken from her sex dreams much sooner. No woman can sleep through the pleasures I can bring them." He pursed his lips as if in thought. "Now that you mention it, maybe you should go out and look for those other females, I'll stay here and enjoy this one."

"You are losing daylight," Jarod snapped, not at all amused with Taylor's suggestion.

A knowing grin washed over his friend's face. "Thought you would see it my way. Besides, if we are lucky I will be bringing back two more females we can enjoy. I always preferred having sex with more than one of them at the same time."

Jarod couldn't help but shake his head in disappointment. The last thing they needed in their camp was females ordering them around.

"We can't afford anyone finding us here. Only bring them back if they are injured and need tending. Make sure to use a blindfold so they won't know our location."

"And if they aren't injured?"

"Take your liberties then scare them away."

"I cannot bring one or both of them back? She says they are her sisters."

"I do not care what she says. We cannot have any women here. They are too dangerous. Once this one is healthy, we will bring her to the edge of The Outer Limits and send her back to where she came from."

Taylor nodded solemnly.

When he started to limp away, guilt slammed into Jarod. His friend's leg had been broken during the Slave Uprising years ago and had never healed properly. Despite the pain that etched his face on a continuous basis, Taylor never complained.

"You should stay the night. Rest your leg. We can both start out in the morning," Jarod called out to him.

"If they are out there and drank too much of the swamp water, they may already be dead from the fever sex dreams. But there is still a chance…"

"Perhaps I should go instead…" He chastised himself for offering to go. The chances were good that if there were others in the Fever Swamps as she'd said, they might also have been infected, and he didn't look forward to orally taking another woman's pleasure cream in order to drain the fever from her body. Truthfully, he preferred to stay here with Piper, just in case she relapsed. Having her succulent pussy in his mouth was a delicacy he couldn't resist.

"I know the swamps like the back of my hand, Jarod. And I know all the shortcuts. So you go ahead and enjoy the female while I am gone."

Taylor winked, and then sauntered off into the surrounding forest.

Jarod exhaled an annoyed breath. He didn't like it when Taylor toyed with him about women. He'd made it perfectly clear he would never go near one again.

What had happened with this woman hadn't been his choice. She'd drank the intoxicating brown water and suffered the dreams. What else should he have done? Left her to die from lack of orgasms? Sucking her pussy cream from her fevered body, and bringing her to orgasm over and over again was the only known cure.

He could have let Taylor do the deeds. Could have let Taylor bring her from the edge of death. But he hadn't been able to allow his friend to care for her. He'd wanted to take care of her himself, and now he was going to suffer for his sympathy toward her.

He should have remembered women inflicted pain, imposed control and only wanted sex from males.

He should have remembered he was free now. And he planned to stay that way. He would never allow another woman to dominate him again. He would never go back to the life of a sex slave.

He would die before he let that happen.

Chapter Two

Piper was having another wild sex dream.

No.

Not a dream.

This was reality, just like the last time.

Someone was squeezing her nipples—twisting them, until the nerve endings cut a deep line of fire straight down to her pussy.

Her eyes fluttered open on a moan.

It was *him*. The one-eyed stranger called Jarod.

He must have been touching her breasts for quite some time because her nipples were on fire, burning and aching with sheer ecstasy. She stifled the urge to whimper her arousal, and through lowered lashes, she studied him closely.

Oh, boy, was he ever built.

Nicely shaped muscles flexed in his biceps as his fingers moved against her throbbing nipples. He hadn't seen her watching him, his one good eye too busy staring at her belly or maybe at her muff.

She swallowed back another whimper as her body blazed beneath his hands. Her gaze wandered to the area between his thighs where she discovered he wore nothing but a small loincloth that did nothing to conceal his large arousal.

A blessedly big arousal!

Unconsciously, she licked her lips and suddenly she couldn't wait to grab onto those powerful male legs, and press her head between *his* thighs and orally take his cock into her mouth.

Oh, my gosh!

What in the world was she thinking? She'd never thought about taking a man's cock into her mouth before.

His one icy-blue eye caught her watching him, and his fingers stilled on her aroused nipples.

"Don't stop," she said hoarsely. "Please, don't stop."

She wanted his magical fingers to keep touching her. Wanted him to make her feel alive, to bring her out of this weakness claiming her.

The way his kissable mouth curved downwards, she wondered what she'd said wrong. He let go of her nipples and abruptly pulled a thin sheet, which appeared to be woven out of black animal hair, over her heaving breasts.

Suddenly embarrassed at having responded so boldly to the stranger, she couldn't stop the heated flush from spreading through her face.

His one eye narrowed warmly at her reaction. Thankfully, he said nothing as he sat down on the edge of the bed beside her and lifted a wooden bowl from the nearby twig table. Steam uncurled from it and drifted into the air.

"Taylor has gone in search for the others."

Relief swept through her.

"Thank you. I appreciate both your and his help."

"If these others are in the swamps, he will find them. He is a very good tracker. No one knows the swamps as good as he does."

Pride and confidence etched his voice, and Piper found his confidence seeping into her system. Yes, if this sexy stranger said his friend would find her sisters then it would happen.

To her surprise, he lifted the spoon and she tried not to make a face at the ugly-looking gray liquid on it.

He came at her mouth with it.

Sweet mercy! He wanted to spoon-feed her?

He was too close. Too sexy. It would be too intimate.

Before she could even attempt to sit up and pretend she wasn't as weak as she felt, his harsh words stopped her cold.

"Lie still. Your wounds are still healing."

"My wounds?"

"Both of your feet were burned."

Her feet? She didn't feel any pain now or earlier. But then again her legs had been hoisted over his massive shoulders while his face had been buried in her quivering cunt.

Don't think about that, *Piper.*

Think about how to get away from this steamy sex hunk who made her feel like she wanted to take a roll in the hay with him, like right now.

She cleared her very dry throat. "How bad are the burns?"

"The soles of your feet got infected. I had to use our entire medical supply to keep from amputating."

Amputation? Her stomach heaved.

"Do not be alarmed. A couple of days rest and you will be fit. In the meantime, you will eat and grow strong."

She grimaced at the earthy-smelling liquid as he touched her lips with the warm spoon.

"What is it?"

"Soup. It is nutritious. Open your mouth."

She did as he instructed and she sipped delicately.

Earthy was her first impression as the salty fluid splashed over her dry tongue. Gooey was her second impression as it slid easily down her parched throat.

It didn't taste bad, but it didn't taste good either.

He dipped the spoon into the bowl again and remained quiet as he spoon-fed her.

The sight of him sitting here beside her, his torso practically naked except for that loincloth partially covering that wondrous bulge, was quickly building a lusty flush throughout her, and making her feel faint at the same time.

His thick black hair was damp and in disarray, as if he'd just taken a dip in a lake or stepped out of a shower, or better yet, stepped straight out of a *Playgirl* magazine. Her body trembled as she imagined the power he had over her should he decide to pull down the sheet again to bare her breasts to him.

But the sexual interest she'd seen gleaming in his eye when he'd touched her nipples earlier was gone, replaced with hostility and bold curiosity.

Speaking of curiosity, where was she, anyway?

She cast a quick gaze around the small room and noted a few big, fat candles held in hangers on the walls. They were lit, their flickering flames casting a buttery glow around the room. Shadows danced across a floor made of small, round saplings strung tightly together by vines. The walls were made of the same material and the low ceiling was obviously straw thatch.

Outside, fireflies flittered past night-darkened windows.

He hadn't said a word while she ate, but the instant she finished the contents of the bowl, his questions began to fly.

"Why were you in the swamp? What is your mission?"

"My mission?"

"Why have you come here?"

What was with the third degree?

"I already told you. To search for my brothers, the Heros."

"So you can kill them." His words were so matter-of-fact she couldn't believe what she'd just heard.

"Are you insane? Why would I want to kill my own brothers?"

"Where do you come from?" he asked.

Good question. How did she tell this guy she came from another planet?

He'd call *her* insane.

Her. A kindergarten teacher who'd left a schoolroom full of cute five-year-old children so she could go on an adventure and travel across the galaxy on a top secret search for her missing brothers.

Heck!

She was the one who was insane.

Carrying on a conversation with a practically nude stranger, allowing him to touch her nipples and eat her cunt? Wanting him to touch her again. Wanting to have wild sex with him.

She couldn't stop her face from flaming yet again at the delightful thoughts.

"Did Cath send you?" The hostility in his voice when he spoke Cath's name made her wonder what horrible things that woman had done to him. Was she the cause of the scars that littered his chest? Was she the reason he was so suspicious of her?

"I...I don't know anyone named Cath. I told you I came in search of my brothers. I have a message for them."

"What message?"

"It's personal. Just tell me where they are. Or at least, bring them here."

"Tell me the message and I will see they get it."

Piper felt herself relaxing into the softness of the bed. "So you do know where they are."

"They are safe and that's the way they will stay."

Obviously, her brothers had found a steadfast friend in this guy. She just wished he'd be a little more cooperative with her. And she wished her bladder would stop filling up so quickly.

She wiggled her bottom a little trying to alleviate the mounting pressure. As if understanding her movements, he reached under the bed.

"I have a bowl you can go in."

"I don't think so!" She wasn't going pee in a bowl with him around. Talk about embarrassing.

"No thanks. Just point me into the right direction and I'll manage."

"That is not possible. Your foot wounds are still recovering."

"I don't feel a thing. Really."

He frowned. "I will carry you outside."

"Gosh, don't sound so thrilled, mister," she muttered.

He stood and his arms reached out to her. She waved him away. "I can walk. Really."

In one fluid motion, he bent over and picked her up, and snuggled her against a broad wall of sculpted chest muscles.

Holy heat wave! It really was getting hot in here.

To her shock, the sheet fell off her body revealing her nudity to him.

Oh, shit!

She looked up and jolted. Heat flamed in his eye as he scrutinized her bared breasts. If looks could make love, he'd be doing it to her right now.

And she wouldn't resist either.

Piper shivered with excitement.

"Are you cold?" he asked quietly.

"No."

Gosh, he had the most amazing blue eye.

She wondered what had happened to his other one? How had he lost it? And once again, she wondered how he had gotten all those scars on his gorgeous chest? Especially the scar that raked across his left nipple, leaving it damaged and puckered, and aching to be sucked.

It wasn't until they were surrounded by darkness that she realized he hadn't bothered to cover her and that he'd carried her outside. Mild air washed against her skin but it did little to douse the arousal shimmering throughout her impassioned body.

Swiss Family Robinson came instantly to mind as she glanced up at the dark outline of an amazing building nestled snugly amongst pine trees.

"We're in a tree house?"

"It is where we live."

"Your friend and you?"

"Yes."

He began to descend and she peered over his shoulder noting the small torches that lit a buttery glow down a set of steep wooden stairs.

Once they cleared the steps, they plunged into semi-darkness. Her eyes quickly accustomed to the new lighting, and she noted moonlight splashing onto a tiny meadow ahead.

A moment later, he placed her feet gently on a patch of moist, cool grass.

Pain shot through her feet and she wavered. She hated the weakness spilling into her limbs and didn't have any choice but to reach out and dig her fingers into his muscular arms.

She could feel the outline of his long, thick cock pressing against his loincloth and into her skin. Her breath caught in her throat and she couldn't stop the whimper of want from escaping her lips.

"Are you not well?" His voice sounded strained, his body tense.

"I'm fine," she lied, as the shape of his hard cock head seared against her lower belly.

Oh, gosh! Please fuck me!

"You can go here."

His voice sounded cold and detached again, urging her to quickly pull away from him.

He wanted her to go here? In front of him?

He made no move to leave. Made no move to look away from her nude body.

And she didn't have the strength to get into an argument with him.

Squatting down, she was quite thankful for the darkness that drifted around them while she tended to business. When she was finished, he handed her some soft leaves to wipe herself, and then quickly swooped her up in his massive arms again.

As they ascended the stairs she couldn't help but respond to the way his muscles flexed against her breast. Or react to his lovely body heat that practically burned her flesh.

As they entered the room, light spilled over his tanned face and every nerve ending jumped to attention at the sight of his lust-blazed eye and at the fact his head was lowering toward her.

Oh, dear!

The instant his hot lips brushed against her mouth, her pussy jerked wonderfully, unleashing a magnificent heat between her legs.

He groaned. It was the most sensual sound she'd ever heard in her life, and she eagerly opened her mouth accepting the hungry thrust of his thick tongue.

Sensations rocked her.

By gosh, the man sure knew how to kiss.

His rough tongue clashed with hers, finding erotic zones she never even knew existed.

His kisses left her breathless and so hot for sex she couldn't even think straight.

Without his hot mouth leaving hers, she suddenly found herself being lowered until her feet shakily hit the floor. The solid heat of his body crushed her against the sapling wall, his knees frantically prodded her legs apart, and she whimpered as she felt his thick, hot shaft, restrained by the loincloth, press intimately against the apex of her thighs.

Her legs weakened at the fierceness of her arousal, and her arms quickly encircled his neck to prevent herself from falling.

He continued to kiss her, encouraging her body to hum with approval at the lusty onslaught of ideas that she actually wanted a stranger to make love to her.

Long masculine fingers slid around her waist and to her backside where he massaged her naked ass cheeks.

In turn, she rubbed her swollen breasts against his hard chest sparking a beautiful friction into her nipples.

His teeth nipped gently at her lower lip making her gasp at the pain. His tongue once again thrust into her mouth clashing violently against her tongue, dominating her, overwhelming her.

Her breath crashed into her lungs as she fought to keep up with his fierce tongue thrusts, to absorb the sensations ripping through her.

Hell's bells! The man knew how to kiss.

When the massive length of his bound cock nestled boldly near the entrance to her cunt, her legs grew weaker, barely supporting her.

His cock felt so unbelievably huge!

His kisses became bolder.

The hands on her ass cheeks massaged harder, pressing her into his hard flesh.

Heated blood surged through her veins. Her soft whimper sliced through the air.

To her disappointment, he broke the kiss.

His breath sounded labored and shallow. Unmistakable desire shone in his eye. Piper's heart exploded against her chest as his cock pulsed against her lower abdomen.

She found herself lowering her head, her mouth tasting and kissing the expanse of his damp chest. Her lips played over the soft dark hairs, the thick raised scars as she eagerly sought the disfigured nipple she'd noticed earlier.

When she drew the tight bud into her mouth, he inhaled sharply. The heat of his fingers sifted tenderly through the strands of her hair. His heart pounded against her lips, his strong masculine scent slammed into her lungs.

Her hands flew over his ribs along his sides running freely down the cleft in his back.

She twirled her tongue around his nipple until it tightened into a hard pebble. Then she bit gently into the dark flesh, making an erotic groan escape past his lips.

It was a primal sound, ripped from his lungs, a wonderful sound that urged her to leave his nipple and travel downward.

Dropping to her knees, she kissed along the fluffy hair that arrowed down over his stomach, following it to the most beautiful bulge she'd ever seen in her life, a full-blown erection that writhed against the loincloth, begging for release.

When her fingers found the ties of his loincloth at the sides of his waist, she pulled gently.

The cloth dropped away.

She swallowed as his long, thick cock sprang free like a wild serpent.

Sweet love!

The man was built like a god!

His shaft stretched straight out at her. At least nine, thick inches long. Shaded an angry purple, she swore she could see the blood pulse through those lovely veins that interwove wildly throughout his thick staff. The mushroom-shaped head burst forth from its sheath, a dot of pre-come at the slit.

Piper licked her lips with anticipation.

A sweet sexual energy rampaged through her making her feel more alive than she'd felt in a long time.

A thick, black nest of curly hair encased his rigid shaft. Blood roared through her ears as she stared at the two egg-shaped globes, large and ready to burst.

His hands tangled in her hair. With firm pressure, he held her head still, and pressed his hard erection against her lips.

Her womb fluttered at the thought of his glorious size penetrating her vagina, stretching her muscles, struggling into her tight slit until he filled her so completely she'd scream out her enjoyment.

A clean scent of soap washed through her nostrils. The thought of him having bathed somewhere, crystal water brushing over his muscular chest as his strong hands rubbed sudsy soap all around his big cock and heavy balls sent a delicious dizzying shot of passion into her system.

Piper parted her lips.

The swollen tip of his hot shaft invaded her mouth.

Her hands found his hard ass cheeks and she held tight, those sizzling muscles contracting beneath her fingertips.

The movement of his hard flesh sliding deeper into her mouth, stretching her lips encouraged her to clamp tightly around his thick erection.

He groaned his approval.

Gosh, she'd never done this before. Never had a cock in her mouth before. What should she do?

As if having a mind of its own, her tongue flung forward and touched the tip of his mushroom-shaped head. He tasted salty, the skin of his cock velvety soft as it covered his rock-hard shaft.

As if reading her thoughts, he muttered softly, "Suck me, woman. Suck me real hard."

Excitement roared through her.

She curled her lips tighter around his hot pulsing flesh; at the same time, her tongue massaged his bulging tip.

He groaned again, a wild animal growl that urged her on. Emptying the air from her cheeks, she created a furious sucking motion. He gasped as if in pain, but his hands kept her head steady as he slowly moved his shaft in and out of her mouth.

She kept the suctioning movements going, her tongue swirling and prodding against the salty tip as she lifted her eyes to stare up at his face.

His one eye was dark as he looked down at her. Dark, and filled with lust and pleasure.

To her surprise, he smiled.

Her heart responded and crashed splendidly against her chest. She drew her lips even tighter around his hot flesh if that was possible, her cheeks hollowing out until she felt the insides of her mouth hugging his rigid cock.

His deep groans echoed throughout the room.

She found herself whimpering in response. Her womb shivered, her vagina muscles clenched around a huge phantom cock as she imagined him sliding into her slit, impaling her.

Her fingers dug harder into his muscular ass cheeks, pulling him closer, urging his cock deeper until he hit the back of her tonsils. For a split second, she thought she might gag, but instinctively relaxed the back of her throat and allowed him to sink even deeper.

Deep throat.

Now she knew the true meaning of the word.

He pulled his cock out slowly, and she sipped at the salty liquid dripping from his slit.

She kept her eyes glued to his face.

His smile had disappeared; his mouth drew tight in a grimace. His eye scrunched closed as he slammed his cock in and out of the tight vacuum her lips and cheeks created.

He thrust his hips forward again; her mouth eagerly sucked his rigid flesh. There was so much more length than what she could take and he seemed to know when to stop and when to pull back.

She'd heard from her friends, even her sisters, who'd said it was better for a woman, or maybe the man himself, to hold the base of his cock to stop him from entering too deeply into her mouth, preventing injury to her when he became lost in the bliss of pleasure.

But this man seemed to possess an amazing control and knew how deep he could go. Seemed to know exactly when to pull back, as if he'd done this to women many times and knew how far he could penetrate with his long shaft.

Mixed emotions shot through her.

Jealousy that he could have serviced many women—hurt that maybe he was only using her for his own sexual release.

Though—most of all—excitement burned through her.

Perhaps he was one of those sex slaves her brothers had mentioned in the message they'd sent back to Earth? Maybe that's why this man had suckled her clit so exquisitely.

Was he a man trained to give pleasure to a woman?

"I am coming!" he groaned.

His tortured voice ripped her from her thoughts. He thrust his hips forward again and buried his rod deep into her throat.

"Oh, Goddess, I am coming!"

He slid his slippery rod out and in again. Long, smooth strokes that slithered erotically against her lips making them swell and quiver with arousal.

His body jerked. His big cock exploded. Hot love juice shot down her throat.

Piper clamped her lips tight and sucked valiantly at his release and listened to his harsh gasps rent the mild night air.

She drained him of his seed. Her taste buds having a feast with the exploding salty liquid as it spurt against her tongue.

She became lost in the sounds of her suckling, the moans of his release until finally he became quiet. With his semi-limp cock still imprisoned by her mouth, she looked up at him; wanting to see the sexual satisfaction on his face, instead she froze.

He looked downright angry.

Furious, as a matter-of-fact.

Had she not done a good enough job in pleasing him?

He sighed wearily and let go of the sides of her head, backing away from her, allowing his cock to slip free from her burning lips.

He picked her up off the floor, cradling her in his arms.

The hot feel of his flesh pressing against her nakedness, the earthy scent of male made Piper swoon.

God! He was going to put her down on the bed and fuck her.

She wanted him with every ounce of her strength. Wanted this stranger's hard, burning cock ramming into her weeping cunt like he'd just filled her mouth.

Sexual desperation made her cry out her distress. He paid her no heed.

He simply lay her on the bed and covered her naked body with the hairy sheet, leaving her fully aroused and so weak, she couldn't even lift her hand to slide it between her legs and bring her hot cunt relief.

"Rest assured," he said coldly. "This will not happen again."

Despite his frosty voice, feverish lust shone bright in his eye. She noted his cock had hardened and straightened once again with arousal.

He turned his broad, scarred back to her, and left her to whimper her sexual frustration to the empty room.

* * * * *

Goddess of Freedom! Was he insane? Fucking a woman's mouth while she was still recovering from the sex fevers and was so weak. He could have hurt her.

Yet, he hadn't been able to stop himself. Hadn't been able to end the torrent of desire ripping through his shaft as she'd kneeled like a goddess between his legs, her silky hands clutching his ass cheeks, her feminine fingers digging deep into his flesh and taking his sex-tormented cock into her mouth.

He'd been totally captivated by the lusty look in her eyes.

Her sparkling green eyes had mesmerized him. Had made him weak to her womanly charms.

All the promises he'd made to himself about remaining distant from the woman, any woman, had simply vanished. Promises he'd made that he would never become a woman's sex slave again had disintegrated as if it meant nothing.

And here he was, servicing himself on an ill woman. It was hard not to turn around and head back up to the room. Agonizing to deny his fingers the silky touch of her soft, long brown hair or caress those delicious womanly curves.

His cock jerked violently at the memory.

Jarod swore.

He was so hard he couldn't wait to plunge his stiff cock deep into her hot cunt.

Clutching his hands into frustrated fists, he halted and looked back up at the tree house with the buttery light spilling from the small windows. No matter how much he wanted to, he couldn't go back up there. If he did, he would fuck her endlessly until this powerful lust burning throughout his feverish body went away.

Clutching his hatred of women back into his heart, Jarod turned around and descended the stairs the rest of the way.

He'd dive into the cool river, that's what he'd do. He doubted anything would dampen the fire the woman's mouth had stoked inside his shaft, but he had to try.

Deep down though, he knew nothing would alleviate the sexual pressure building inside his body. Nothing would extinguish this intense yearning to couple with the woman. Nothing would help him but plunging his now rock-hard cock deep into her spasming channel.

Chapter Three

Much to Piper's annoyance, Jarod kept her mostly in bed the entire next day. Coming and going only to make sure she ate and to carry her down to go to the bathroom. He seemed distant and cold to the point Piper almost cried out her sexual frustration every time she saw him.

Why she was reacting like some deprived hussy was beyond her. She'd never acted this way on Earth. Back home she'd possessed a level, calm head dating men who were safe, men who had a solid job, a secure future. A man who would be a great provider for their kids.

In essence, she realized she'd only dated men who were boring. This guy was totally opposite of what she'd always looked for in a potential mate.

He was well built, in a natural sort of way. Not the hard muscles of guys who worked out in a gym, but sensually shaped muscles from hard physical labor.

What kind of labor, she didn't have a clue. Obviously, he didn't have a job in an office, nor did he live in a nice house. Heck! He lived in a tree house.

Like Tarzan.

And she was Jane.

Jane of the jungle who ached for another searing kiss from him, Jane who needed to feel his thick rod pulse in her mouth again, craved to have that gorgeous cock stabbing between her legs.

Most of all, she wished she could pry away those layers of anger and maybe even get rid of the hatred toward her. At least she figured it to be hatred, and she wanted to find out what haunted miseries glowed in his eye.

By evening, Taylor hadn't come back, and Jarod was obviously getting worried. He hadn't said anything about it when he'd checked in on her, but during his absences she'd sneak out of bed on tender feet to look out the windows of the tree house.

On more than one occasion, she discovered Jarod standing twenty feet below staring into the jungle, a frown on his face.

His tormented face echoed her thoughts.

Where was Taylor?

Had he found her sisters? Were they hurt badly? Is that why he was taking so long?

She knew both of her sisters had been injured. How badly, she'd no idea. They'd all had cuts and scrapes and bruises, and had fought to get out of the brown, smelly water and fingerlike weeds that had threatened to drown them instead of tending to any injuries.

Maybe Taylor hadn't found them and he was widening his search?

Anguish clutched at her heart every time she heard Jarod's footsteps climb the stairs for fear he might have bad news. The anguish quickly turned to lust. A dark lust that she figured kept coming at her because she needed some way to distract herself about the possible fate of her sisters.

She remembered taking a psychology class in university. Remembered the theories of how a person would do the oddest things in order to distract himself or herself while waiting for potentially bad news.

She just hadn't ever thought she'd go the sexual route.

Every time he arrived and didn't have any news, she frantically stuck to her motto.

No news is good news.

That night she wished he would come to her. She wished they could pick up where they left off, if only so she could keep her mind off her anxiety about her sisters.

But he didn't show up. It was just as well. Sleeping with a guy just to keep herself occupied was never a good idea. Being sexually attracted to him however was another story.

And boy was she sexually attracted to the guy.

Every time she looked at his face, it reminded her of waking up with his head buried between her thighs. His tongue expertly teasing her clit, his tongue thrusting in and out of her while she'd lain helpless on the bed.

Not to mention how her body burned at the sight of the exquisite bulge trying to hide behind that loincloth.

Piper blew out an aroused breath. The man looked sexy as sin.

His cock had felt unbelievably great in her mouth. She could only imagine what he'd do to her when they finally slept together. There was no doubt in her mind they eventually would, if she hung around here for much longer.

That night she slept fitfully and dreamed of Jarod. Dreamed of his magnificent body standing between her widespread legs. His large swollen cock held in his hand as he guided himself toward her, his balls heavy with his seed, she herself responding with a sexual fever she couldn't seem to extinguish.

The next morning it was the hot sunshine that streamed through a window and washed over her, prodding her awake from her dreams.

When her eyes flicked open, she knew instantly Jarod had left.

Knew it by the bucket of water and the food he'd left on the nearby table, and by the overwhelming silence that drifted through the tree house.

To her shock, she discovered a long gleaming knife, its blade stuck into the sapling floor beside her bed.

A tingle of fear shimmied up her back.

He'd left her the knife for protection. But protection from whom? Or what?

Using a cloth and a green-looking bar of soap, which oddly smelled of fresh peppermint, she used the cool water from the bucket and quickly washed herself. When she was finished, she felt quite refreshed and quickly wrapped the thin sheet around her, grabbed some fruit and stood. Testing her feet on the floor, she smiled. They weren't sore at all. Amazingly enough, she didn't feel weak anymore either.

Stepping outside onto the veranda, she couldn't stop herself from inhaling a deep breath of fresh, sweet forest air. This was the first time she'd been out of the tree house on her own and without Jarod around to distract her.

Immediately she noticed something she hadn't seen before. Extending from the sapling veranda to the back of her tree house was a thin narrow bridge stretching toward other tree houses nestled in other nearby trees.

Biting into a juicy peach, she savored the delicious sweetness and walked across the rickety bridge toward the nearest hutch. There was nothing special about it. It looked the same as the one she'd been in over the past few days. It consisted of a handmade mattress on a makeshift sapling bench, a couple of wooden hooks tied to a wall and some wooden bowls hung from them.

It was the next tree house, or at least what she figured to be a tree house, so hidden in the dense foliage high above the other two, that she almost didn't see it except for the rope ladder dangling in the warm breeze.

Managing to climb up the awkward creation, she discovered what she perceived as the men's lookout.

A platform allowed her to see for miles and miles across the tops of the forest trees. Way in the distance a row of hills shimmered in the hazy sunshine. To her left she could even see what she perceived as the creepy swamp Taylor and Jarod had found her in.

Littered by skeleton trees, their dark branches were draped in dripping brown moss—the swamp seemed to stretch for miles.

Piper enjoyed the view for a long time, allowing the warm breeze to blow against her naked body as she ate the other fruit she'd brought along with her, and hoped against hope she would see a smoke signal of some kind from one of her sisters.

None came.

Her eyes began to burn with weariness and her heart clenched with anguish as the sun sailed high in the blue sky, scorching her skin with fire. Finally, she decided it would be better to head down into the coolness of the tree house to take a nap.

As she climbed down, she couldn't help but notice a tattered bag hanging off a tree limb beneath the platform she'd just been sitting on.

How odd. Why would they store something way up here?

Reaching out, she managed to grab it.

A few moments later as she sat on her bed, she opened it and her blood froze.

Nestled inside were two familiar mugs. Ceramic mugs. Mugs with the words NASA written on them in bold letters.

Had Jarod and Taylor taken these mugs from her brothers? Had the two men killed them and disposed of their bodies?

Or had her brothers broken NASA's protocol of keeping a low profile for a reason?

Many other scenarios began running through her head.

Shit!

The questions were endless.

When either Jarod or Taylor returned, she'd be sure to squeeze the truth out of them.

* * * * *

This was the exact spot where they had discovered Piper, Jarod thought as he surveyed the area.

Gray mist floated eerily over the brown mirror-like water. Large dead trees, their twisted branches clawing toward the sky, were draped with strands of brown moss that glowed eerily in the late afternoon sunshine.

Nothing else grew here.

No flowers.

No grass.

Only rotting logs, giant boulders and those eerie-looking trees draped in moss.

Jarod shivered at the thought of Piper dying here all alone if he and Taylor hadn't come along when they had. It was around this time of day they'd found her. They'd been following the footprints of the notorious black bear that had killed several males over the last couple of years. The bear had led them into the Fever Swamps, wetlands that stretched for miles in every direction.

He'd come upon her naked, pale body quite by accident. Taylor had totally missed her as he'd been intent on following the bear tracks.

Jarod however had caught sight of a pale arm moving ever so slightly amongst the moss-strewn rocks. Shock had rippled through him the instant he'd found her. His cry of surprise had attracted his friend's help. They'd quickly checked her limp body for broken bones and discovered the infected burns on her feet.

Jarod hadn't thought she would make it.

Her body was too hot.

She had awakened briefly and when he'd seen those pretty green eyes laced with fever, something beautiful had shifted inside Jarod's heart, and he wanted so desperately for her to live.

And she had.

He groaned as he remembered the night he'd carried her in his arms down the curling steps into the meadow where she'd relieved herself. The moonlight striking her pale skin had been a vision he would treasure forever. And the way her innocent eyes had sparkled at him as he'd carried her back up to the tree house. Her body finally free of the fever but heated with restrained passion.

He hadn't thought twice about kissing her. Hadn't thought twice about refusing to have her succulently shaped mouth devouring his swollen cock.

Yet shame assailed him for having a taste of her charms because he didn't think he could stop himself from having her again and again until she was so exhausted she would never be able to escape him. He forced his thoughts away from Piper and onto Taylor as he once again surveyed the area.

There was no sign that he had even been here. Not that he had expected to find any clues, Taylor being the expert that he was in covering his tracks. But Jarod had hoped his friend had somehow slipped up, leaving the tiniest little piece of evidence that he had been here and that he was safe.

He found nothing.

Guilt ripped through him at how easily he'd let Taylor go out alone. Every year his leg got worse, and if he wasn't careful he could be captured by one of the Yellow Hair hunting parties. Those women were beautiful blondes but fatal for males.

Males never lived to tell about how well those women performed in bed for it was a tradition amongst the Yellow Hairs to kill and eat all males after they fucked them. Those women were the biggest customers of The Breeders in obtaining males. He couldn't help but worry that one day Taylor would end up getting captured by the Yellow Hairs and eaten.

Jarod inhaled wearily and headed off into another direction to continue his search for Taylor.

* * * * *

The creak on the steps leading to the tree house sifted through the layers of her late afternoon nap, prodding Piper awake.

Heart hammering violently against her chest, she blinked her eyes open and listened intently.

Another creak followed.

Shoot! She'd never noticed the steps creaking when Jarod had come up.

Obviously, it wasn't him, and that meant she needed to get the hell out of here.

And she needed to do it fast.

Trying to keep the terror sinking into her at bay, she yanked the sheet around her nude body, struggled out of bed and quickly padded barefoot to a back window. She'd climb outside and stand on the narrow ledge she'd noticed before. Hopefully the intruder would leave when he couldn't find anyone home.

She was halfway out the window when a man's voice made her freeze.

"Going somewhere?"

Immediately she recognized the voice of Taylor, the man who'd caught Jarod with his head between her legs.

Oh, how embarrassing!

"Do not be frightened. I will not hurt you. Come down from there."

Trying hard to douse the intense heat flaming her face, Piper climbed down from the sill, and reluctantly turned to face the stranger who was limping over to her bed. His arms bulged beautifully as he flung a rather tattered-looking knapsack off his back and deposited it on the mattress.

Tarzan was her first impression of the guy.

With feathery brown locks of hair that reached his massive shoulders, he possessed unruly bangs that hung just above a pair of a very nice pair of warm brown eyes.

He was quite tall.

At least a head taller than Jarod.

And like Jarod, he had whip marks all over his bare chest and abdomen, and wore nothing but a breechclout, quite similar to Jarod's; and like Jarod's, it didn't do much to conceal a thick bulge between his powerful-looking thighs.

A great fit for her sister, Kayla, was her second impression. Kayla loved well-endowed hunks and her compassionate side always drew her to injured men, which he was, if his limp was an indication.

"Did you find Kayla and Kinley?"

He ignored her question. His gaze was directed toward the knife Jarod had left stuck in the sapling floor.

"Where is Jarod?" he asked.

"He went out looking for you."

Her tension eased when Taylor chuckled heartily. "That male never stops worrying about me. He knows very well I can take care of myself."

"Did you find my sisters?"

His full lips dipped into a frown, and a strong knot of apprehension curled inside of Piper's stomach as his gaze moved from the knife back to her.

"I covered a large portion of the perimeter of the swamp, but not all of it. I do believe at least one of your sisters is alive and well."

Thank God.

"Where is she? Why didn't you bring her back?"

"There was one set of female footprints near where we found you. I tried to follow, but she was good in covering her tracks. As if she didn't want to be found."

Covering her tracks? How odd. Why would one of her sisters do something like that? And which sister was it?

Could it be her identical twin, Kinley?

Or Kayla, the baby sister of the family?

Kinley, older than Piper by two minutes was Piper's total opposite behavior-wise.

Where both of them were petite with small breasts and had long, brown curly hair and green eyes, Piper had been a quiet geek of a teenager who preferred to spend time babysitting kids and playing with her pets. Kinley, on the other hand, was outgoing and so popular with the guys that Piper had envied her for the confidence she possessed when it came to men. Most of all, she wished for Kinley's sexual experiences, of which her sister had admitted were many and varied.

Kinley had been in her first year of studying to be a crime scene investigator when they'd received the secret messages from their brothers in their farewell video explaining that they were remaining behind on the top secret planet named Paradise. Not too long after that, Kinley had become quieter, less friendly, more withdrawn. Piper had attributed it to the fact that she was worried about their brothers stranded here on a planet ruled by women.

Then she'd surprised Piper with her suggestion of getting some fast, heavy-duty astronaut training through some of their brothers' astronaut friends who would help outfit them for a journey to kick their brothers' asses and get them to come back home.

Piper had accepted the idea immediately.

And then there was sweet Kayla.

The serious sister. The one who wanted to help suffering animals.

She'd been in her second year of veterinary school when she'd learned Kinley and Piper were secretly training to come to Paradise. Without warning, she'd quit school so she could join them on their mission to search for their brothers.

Now at least one of them was wandering around in a cesspool of a swamp that gave, if what Jarod had said, feverish sex dreams. She could be injured, and she was all alone.

She wished she should feel if Kinley was alive, but they'd never had that bond that some twins shared.

"I am sorry I could not bring back more fruitful news. I do plan on searching another section in the morning. I did notice your skin is pale and not used to the sunshine. I assume you are one of the few women who prefer to wear clothing, so I retrieved some for you."

He opened the knapsack and she saw what looked like clothes inside.

"Clothes! I could kiss you," Piper laughed, as she settled onto the bed and stuck her hand into the knapsack.

"I wouldn't stop you," Taylor chuckled. "Unfortunately, Jarod would not approve."

The tiniest zip of curiosity and excitement prodded Piper to ask, "Why not?"

Taylor shifted uncomfortably and stared at his feet. "He enjoyed you many times while you were in your fever sex dreams, trying to cure you and bring you back to the land of the living, and I'm sure he's enjoyed you since I've been gone. I believe despite his not wanting to, he has grown somewhat attached to you."

Piper's cheeks flamed.

Exactly how often *had* Jarod enjoyed her while she'd slept?

Soft glimpses erupted into her memories. Visions of the one-eyed man brushing his lips against her fevered face — of tender touches between her aching legs.

"By the way your face is red, I presume I am right about Jarod enjoying you."

He said it so matter-of-factly, as if the topic of sex between them was purely natural, that Piper could only stare at him in astonishment.

"I'm glad he is finally interacting with a woman. He says he hates them for what they put him through. But a male should not blame all women for what a few did to him. Besides, we cannot live long without a woman's pleasure." He turned around giving her an awesome view of the whip scars on his broad muscular back as he limped toward the door. "There are sandals inside the pack to protect your feet. Please put them on and then come down below. I will make us food."

By golly, to her surprise, her stomach growled with hunger. "Okay. Thanks, I'll be down in a minute."

Gosh, why couldn't Jarod be as handsome and sweet, and easygoing as this guy? On the other hand, maybe she'd rather Jarod be the way he was, rough-looking with animal magnetism, because as she'd just discovered, she wasn't as sexually attracted to sweet guys like Taylor.

So, Jarod had saved her life, had he? Strange behavior from a man who supposedly hated women. That certainly accounted for his gruff attitude toward her and why he didn't trust her, and thought she was on a mission to destroy her brothers. If Jarod hated women so much as Taylor claimed, then why would he "suck" the poison out of her?

Good question.

Maybe she'd ask him someday, if she hung around long enough to get the nerve.

Returning her attention to the knapsack, she eagerly pulled the items out one by one. Her enthusiasm dropped quickly.

Taylor called these things clothes?

There were two pairs of tiny thong thingies that were virtually see-through, and would most definitely show off her ass cheeks to Jarod, and give him a bird's eye view of her pussy. Not to mention these silky see-through tank top-like cloths would give Jarod an eyeful of her breasts and nipples.

She didn't know whether she should be excited or sad.

Sad that she couldn't seem to shed her sexual inhibitions even millions of miles from Earth. She should just cut herself loose and enjoy the sexual freedom on this planet while she was here.

She giggled as she held up the tiny tank tops.

At least there was no one here who could report her to the principal for dressing inappropriately. No students who would see her. Just a couple of gorgeous-looking wild hunks living like Tarzan in a tree house, and one man in particular that she wouldn't mind showing her assets off to.

Sure, her boobs weren't big but they would fit in a man's hands if he chose to cup them.

She shivered with excitement upon remembering the scorching lust that had burned deep inside her womb at the intense way Jarod's fingers had twisted and tweaked her nipples the other day when she'd awakened.

She'd already come out of her so-called fever sex dreams. He'd had no reason to fondle her. So why had he?

Piper giggled, and hugged the delicious clothing close to her chest. Oh, yes, she sure wanted Jarod's hot hands touching her flesh again. Wanted to have his head buried between her legs, his tongue flicking against her clit and maybe more.

What better way to tease Jarod than to wear these? What better way to give him ideas that she wanted to have a little wild liberated sex?

Abruptly her thoughts returned to her missing sisters and brothers.

She frowned.

Time to stop her silly fantasizing and pump Taylor for more information. If what he said was true, and he was heading out tomorrow to look for Kayla and Kinley then she wanted to go with him.

Quickly she donned the white see-through thong and a sheer, pretty pink tank top that did nothing to hide her sexual assets.

Gosh! She'd kill for a mirror.

Sliding her sore feet into the comfy shoes, which were apparently made of some sort of soft, brown leather, Piper headed down to meet with Taylor.

She found him feeding some sticks into a small smokeless campfire in the middle of a clearing not too far away from the tree house village. Sizzling on a stone-like grate were three thick slabs of what looked oddly similar to beef jerky and a handful of miniature sunny-side up eggs.

Piper's mouth watered at the tantalizing aroma.

"Food will be finished in a moment. Have a seat, there is water in the bucket for you to drink."

Piper noted two wooden mugs next to the pail.

"Actually I'd prefer the NASA mugs my brothers gave you, or did you steal them?"

His shoulders stiffened at her remark. Obviously, he knew what she was talking about.

"Those mugs were given to Jarod. He does not steal," he said without looking at her.

"I'm sorry but I don't know if I can believe you. There's no proof my brothers are even alive. Jarod isn't saying anything, so it's up to you to make me believe that you two didn't murder my brothers in cold blood and steal from them."

Although she was accusing him of murder, deep down she didn't think they would have hurt her brothers. Taylor's warm brown eyes were not that of a cold-blooded killer. And the protective way Jarod had reacted when she'd inquired about her brothers wasn't the way of someone trying to hide a murder.

Taylor turned from the fire he'd been tending. Disappointment gleamed in his eyes, and the severe frown he toted made her think she'd just offended him.

Too bad buddy, but it was time to get tough in her quest for answers.

"Yet you believe me when I say I found footsteps in the swamp. I could be lying. I could have found those two women and killed them."

Sweet mercy! Had he killed them? Fear for their safety just about ripped her heart apart.

"I do not lie," he said. "I did not harm them and your brothers are safe."

Piper literally sagged with relief, and he turned the sizzling jerky to the other side. "As I said, at least one of your sisters is alive. I suspect both of them are."

"Then please tell me where I can find my brothers so we can go and find them."

"It will be up to Jarod to tell you where the Heros are."

Son of a bitch!

"Forget Jarod. You tell me!"

He shrugged his shoulders. "I cannot. I have always been blindfolded when I go there. You must ask Jarod to lead you. He is the only one who knows."

Piper groaned her frustration. "He doesn't trust me. He won't tell me anything. He thinks I'm here to kill them."

"Are you?"

"What is with you two paranoids? Why would someone want to kill my brothers? They're sweet. They would never hurt anyone. They don't have a mean bone in their bodies."

"This is the reason we cannot put their lives in jeopardy. They are too innocent of the ways of the women here."

A twinge of compassion zipped through Piper as Taylor winced when he sat down on a stump of wood and stretched his bad leg out in front of him.

"Besides, they are male and they speak," he continued. "Two good reasons for a woman to want them dead. They also have death bounties on their heads, as do Jarod and I."

"Death bounties!"

Sweet Pete! What kind of a planet was this? Obviously, NASA had made a big mistake in naming this place Paradise.

"Am I to understand you come from the same place as these other males?" he asked as he began to massage his upper thigh. A very muscular thigh that might have turned her on if she wasn't already sexually attracted to Jarod.

Piper blinked in shock.

Heavens! She was not attracted to Jarod!

"Of course we come from the same place. Now do you mind telling me how I can get to them?" *So I can get the hell out of here before Jarod comes back.*

Taylor grimaced as he kept rubbing his upper thigh.

"What's the matter? Did you twist something in your leg? I noticed you limping earlier."

"It is not twisted," he snapped, pain quite evident in his voice. "It just bothers me sometimes when I walk too long."

Sympathy and guilt washed over her. He'd walked too long because of her request to search for her sisters.

"Oh…well…let me try and help. I took a couple of courses in erotic-massage, maybe I can bring you some relief."

Erotic massage courses with her boring ex-boyfriend who she'd had to drag to the courses, and he hadn't even wanted to practice on her when they'd finished the classes. Not even once. At least on this planet, she was getting some hot and heavy sexual attention. No wonder she was responding so violently to Jarod.

Piper sighed, and plopped herself on the ground in front of him.

Ignoring the surprised look on his face, she splayed her feet on each side of outthrust legs, grabbed his foot, pulling a leg forward between hers. When her hands slid to the area of his thigh where he'd been rubbing, she immediately noted the tenseness in his muscles there.

"Your leg is all tied up in knots. Obviously, your problem has been going on for some time. Jarod shouldn't have asked you to go look for my sisters."

"Jarod is useless in the swamps," Taylor groaned, as she began to rub against a particularly large knot.

"This is a trigger point, that's why it hurts," she explained, as she eased off the pressure a little. "What you need is a professional massage therapist."

"Massage? Only women are allowed massages."

"That's crap. Men have muscles, too."

A shocked look flashed across his face at her words, and Piper realized her mistake. She was giving away too much by showing him compassion. Obviously, he wasn't used to it. If she wasn't careful she'd screw NASA's protocol about them having to keep a low profile on this planet. But NASA didn't know they were here. Their trip had been privately funded by her brothers' astronaut friends who'd been sworn to secrecy about this mission because as far as NASA was concerned, Paradise was a deadly planet, and was now off-limits because of her brothers' video reports that came back to Earth with the abandoned spaceship.

"So why don't you just tell me where my brothers are? I'll go get them and they can help us to look for my sisters."

She lifted a cup of water from the bucket and splashed it on Taylor's leg making it slippery so she could increase her pressure. Taylor grimaced, and then sighed as she felt a knotted muscle literally disintegrate in his thigh.

Her fingers stilled on his warm flesh. "There's more relief like that if you tell me what I want to know."

"It is too dangerous for you to travel there alone. You will wait for Jarod."

"I don't know when he'll be back, and like I've said, he's made it quite clear he won't help me. Why don't you just tell me and I'll strike out tonight." She picked up a nearby stick and handed it to him. "Please, draw me a map of how to get there. At least that'll give me an idea of how long it would take."

"You are a determined woman," he smiled, and accepted the stick then groaned as she began to knead against the next trigger point higher up on the inside of his thigh.

"Sorry. It will feel better when I'm finished."

"It feels better already. You must do this to Jarod. Especially to his cock."

Oh, God!

"He would most appreciate it, especially since he has gone without a woman for over two years."

Two years!

Piper swallowed back the excitement at this newest bit of information. The man hated women and hadn't been with one for over two years, except for the other night when she'd gone down on him. Now she understood his anger. It hadn't been directed at her, but at himself because he'd allowed himself to be pleasured by a woman.

Not just any woman, but her.

Piper shivered with excitement.

Just imagine the restrained sexual energy burning inside him!

Whew! It sure was getting warm out here.

With the stick she'd handed him, Taylor poked a small circle into the dirt beside where she sat. "We are here," he said, and then moved the stick through the dirt weaving a couple of dips.

"The quickest way from here is to follow the rising sun which would lead you straight through this first valley, then over the hills and into the second valley. Or you can go via the Fever Swamps but it is longer from this area. I do not know the exact location but Jarod told me your brothers are in the far corner of the second valley beneath some large cliffs, but as I said, it is very dangerous."

"Too dangerous for a woman alone." Jarod's crisp voice broke through the stillness of the early evening making Piper jolt.

Looking up she found him standing right beside her.

Good grief! The man walked around like a ghost. She hadn't even heard him sneaking up on her.

He stared down at her with a combination of fury and lust in his one eye. Despite his anger, his appreciative gaze roamed freely over the so-called clothing Taylor had brought her.

She almost cried out at the intensity of desire shining in his eye as a soft heat shimmered through her. Her nipples suddenly felt hard and achy; her breasts throbbed and felt swollen, and terribly heavy. She resisted the urge to reach up and cover her breasts from his bold view.

By golly, she'd forgotten how sexy that black patch made him look, and the luscious way his chest was heavily laced with muscles and scars. Scars she wanted to kiss and touch, and sit on and grind her wet pussy into, while he eagerly sucked her nipples into his mouth.

She swallowed back the embarrassment at being on such a carnal display, reminding herself that he was a stranger, and she deserved to indulge in a savage little fantasy of wanting this man between her legs again.

As if he knew what she was thinking, his gaze dropped down to the apex of her widespread legs where she had planted Taylor's foot to the ground. She found herself following his gaze, and realized the way she sat with her legs widespread she was giving both men quite the intimate view of her pussy.

A wonderful zip of arousal shot through her, and she couldn't stop the slight inhalation of breath at her sweet reaction.

Snap out of it, girl!

"I can handle myself," Piper bristled.

Jarod ignored her remark and turned his attention to Taylor.

"Did you see anything?"

She didn't miss the fact that the bulge hidden behind Jarod's loincloth was getting much, much bigger.

When she restarted her exploration of Taylor's powerfully built thigh, she noticed the way Jarod's eye strayed to where her fingers massaged his knotted muscles. Much to her amusement, his eye narrowed and his lips tightened with what she could only perceive to be more anger.

Good. The man deserved to get a little irritated for not being nice to her.

"I saw one set of female footprints carefully concealed. Did you?" Taylor asked.

"Yes. I saw them as I was heading back. I also found a dead fire. I assume it didn't belong to you."

"I didn't make a fire. I know the rules."

Jarod nodded.

"What rules?" Piper asked.

Once again Jarod ignored her question and said, "I discovered why she was covering those footsteps. She had a struggle with a couple of males. There was blood."

"No," Piper whispered, as shock seeped into her bones.

Jarod's hand gently cupped her shoulder in reassurance. "Rest easy, she escaped unharmed. It was one of the males who was injured. I followed her trail until she entered the river system. Then I lost her. If she stays in the river, she will be safe. I also discovered a second set of woman's footsteps running near the tip of the swamp."

"I didn't get that far," Taylor acknowledged.

Piper's head snapped up. "It has to be Kayla. She's a jogger. Did you follow them?"

"I followed her tracks until she met up with a group of women and joined their party. I decided to return."

"Both women are alive as I suspected," Taylor commented.

Piper exhaled a sigh of relief. Thank God! Her sisters were okay. Now all she had to do was find them.

"Perhaps this one might have been better off dead." Jarod said quietly, a severe frown marring his face.

"What the hell is that supposed to mean?"

"The one I followed may be in trouble. I believe the group of women she met up with are The Breeders."

Taylor cursed quietly.

"The Breeders?" she whispered. With a handle like that, it was easy to figure out what they did for a living.

Taylor frowned, "The Breeders are a large group of women. They steal males from hubs and sell them to other hubs. Or they use males to impregnate women and sell the babies. I have heard they have recently sold a woman or two to the Death Valley Boys."

"Who are the Death Valley Boys?" she asked.

Now that she knew her sisters were alive, her curiosity about this planet and its occupants was growing by the second.

A strange look passed between the two men.

"You don't want to go near them," Jarod said tightly. "But if they are planning to sell her to the Death Valley Boys then she is safe for a while as they put her through training."

"Training? What kind of training?"

Again, that strange looked passed between them. It made her nervous, and for a second she wished she hadn't asked the question.

"Sex slave training," Taylor whispered. "Inside a week she'll be begging to be fucked by any male, even one or maybe all of the Death Valley Boys."

"Sex slave training?" Piper echoed not believing her baby sister would be subjected to something like that.

"I will go after her at first light," Taylor said quickly.

"No, it is too dangerous," Jarod growled.

"The hell it is!" Piper snapped back at him. "My sister is not going to become some sex slave. I'm going with Taylor when he heads out."

"I'd prefer you didn't. I can travel much quicker alone," Taylor said with a frown.

"But your leg is—"

"Please do not argue. The quicker I can get to her, the faster I can get her out. You would only slow me down."

This time Jarod didn't argue, but she could tell by the way the muscles twitched in his jaw that he was getting angrier by the minute. Suddenly he squatted down beside her and wiped out the makeshift map Taylor had drawn in the dirt for her.

She didn't protest.

A good memory on her part did have its advantages. If Taylor's map had been accurate, she'd have no trouble finding the valley where her brothers were staying.

As a small way of payback, Piper moved her hands higher along Taylor's muscular thigh, and much closer to the lovely bulge pressing against his loincloth. From the corner of her eye she noticed Jarod follow her hand movements and didn't miss the curious smile tilting Taylor's lips.

"Your hands are giving me quite a hard-on, Piper," Taylor sighed.

Oh, my God!

She couldn't stop her face from flaming yet again. Despite her embarrassment at his words, she forced herself to keep her fingers kneading at his tense muscles.

Jarod's jaws clenched tighter as he stared at her hands sliding over Taylor's flesh, practically nudging against his erection.

"If you keep going further up, I am sure I can give you a good time tonight." Taylor threw her a teasing wink — at least she thought it was a teasing wink.

With a huff which she perceived as frustration, Jarod stood.

"Too bad Jarod came back so soon. Who knows where your fantastic massage would have led."

"Then I had best leave you two to find out," Jarod snapped. "I bid you good night."

Before Piper could so much as blink, he stomped away.

"Must have been something I said," Taylor grinned.

"Must have," Piper mused as she watched Jarod tramp up the steep steps and disappear into the other tree house that he was apparently sharing with Taylor while she stayed in his.

She returned her attention to her patient.

"Will you really go and rescue my sister?"

"I will." He wiggled his leg. "Seems whatever you have done has loosened me up."

"But isn't it dangerous for you with those Breeder people wandering around catching men?"

"I'll only get caught if I want to get caught." His grin widened. "Why? Are you worried for me?"

"Actually, no. I'm more worried about Kayla, if you get her out. She has this thing for big guys," she giggled, and began massaging his thigh again. Her fingers immediately found another knotted muscle to work on.

"If she is half as beautiful as you are, she will have every reason to be worried."

Piper's head snapped up at his serious tone.

Dark lust brewed in Taylor's eyes. Instinctively, she knew he was telling her the truth. If his sex-starved gaze was an indicator then Kayla was in deep trouble when he caught up to her.

Chapter Four

Early the next morning, red-hot anger roared through Jarod as he studied the message Taylor had scrawled into the dirt near the fire pit.

Back in a few days, it read.

Damn the Goddess of Freedom!

When Taylor had turned in for the night, he'd tried to talk some sense into him, but he hadn't budged on his plan to look for the other woman. He'd planned on waking extra early and trying again to talk Taylor out of his crazy idea, but his friend had fled the tree house sometime in the night.

If the Breeders had her, Taylor would need much more than one male to get her out of their top security encampment. Besides, he wasn't totally convinced Piper was telling them the truth. For all he knew, she was here to kill the Hero brothers. Until he was sure, he'd planned on keeping a constant eye on her, and secretly sending Taylor for the Hero brothers who would confirm or deny her story, and help them rescue the missing women.

But he couldn't do anything now because Piper and Taylor were both gone.

Obviously, they had left together.

Last night he'd caught the quick wink Taylor had given her after his comment if Jarod hadn't come back so soon he would have made her happy.

He'd assumed it had been a teasing remark aimed at him.

Apparently he'd been mistaken!

His anger boiled to a higher degree as he imagined Taylor and Piper in each other's arms.

Why that should bother him so much, he had no clue. But when he caught up to them, he was going to…

Going to what?

What else did he expect his friend to do? He'd told Taylor he could take her for himself, and he wasn't the type of male who could stay away from sex for very long. He'd obviously taken Jarod seriously and taken him up on the offer.

And what about Piper?

She'd enjoyed massaging his thigh a little too much last night. Not to mention virtually touching his sex, as well as giving them quite the view of her pussy.

Women!

They were all the same. Interested in one thing.

Sex.

To hell with them! They could have each other!

* * * * *

The sickening stench of death made Piper gag as she surveyed the array of wooden scaffolds containing human bodies in various stages of decomposition.

Dammit!

She must have taken a wrong turn somewhere. Taylor hadn't mentioned any graveyard. And by the awful smell sifting through the late afternoon air, it was still in use.

Lovely.

Just lovely.

After watching Taylor sneak out of the tree house in the wee hours of the morning, she'd decided to make the trek to find her brothers on her own. If she'd hung around then Jarod would only have been in her way, distracting her with his gorgeous muscles and that succulently large cock.

Besides, he didn't trust her anyway, why stick around and get insulted?

So she'd grabbed a tattered knapsack, stuffed it with some food and water she'd located in the tree house she'd been housed in then snuck away before Jarod had awakened.

Now as the hot afternoon sun beat down on her she wished for some sunscreen, some sunglasses and a proper topical map so she could at least figure out how big this cemetery was.

Taylor had said she needed to go through two valleys.

This was the first one. The other one had to be over the next set of hills in the far distance.

Gosh! She hadn't realized a valley could be so large and so wide.

Grimacing, she stared at the nearest white skeletons lain out on the wooden scaffolds. The scaffolds were decorated with various bird feathers. Each had a pole at the head side with bone necklaces and colorful pieces of cloth and feathers hanging from them.

She'd seen burial grounds like this in the movies. Never in real life. Weren't these types of places full of evil spirits or something?

A tinge of uneasiness slipped up her spine as she squinted into the haze drifting over the cemetery. It seemed to stretch for miles in both directions. Maybe she'd get lost if she went straight through? Maybe it would never end?

Perhaps she could go around?

No, she couldn't do that. It would take too long. She only had enough water and food for a couple of days.

Besides Kinley and Kayla didn't have the time for her to pussyfoot around.

She needed to stop being such a chicken and just go straight through the cemetery. She could probably reach the bottom of the faraway hills tonight, climb them the next day and get into the next valley the day after.

A shot of happiness filled her at the thought of reuniting with her brothers. What a hoot! Would they ever be surprised and shocked to find out their sisters had tracked them down.

She hadn't seen Joe, Ben or Buck in over two years and now that she was so close to them she couldn't stand the thought of a silly burial ground slowing her down.

Mind made up, she swept the packsack off the ground and walked further into the disgusting smell of the decomposing bodies. With her free hand, she clamped her nose and concentrated on breathing through her mouth, at least that way she wouldn't be able to smell anything.

Yes, she could do this.

All she needed was to keep her eyes straight ahead and not look at the skeletons and corpses. She would simply keep her mind off her current predicament by thinking about her brothers, and how she'd kick their butts for staying back here on this godforsaken planet and scaring the daylights out of the family.

When NASA had told them her brothers' spaceship had come back without them along with a taped message stating they had contracted some sort of deadly plague on the planet, everyone had been shocked and upset to say the least.

Thankfully, NASA had given them a copy of the videodisk her brothers had made especially for the family. The trio had seemed healthy enough when they'd revealed they'd been infected with a toxic plague that would eventually kill them.

They'd seemed sincere in warning NASA not to come for them. Explaining their scientific experiments revealed all kinds of deadly diseases and toxins that were fatal to humans.

Yet, the section where her brothers had left farewells to the family had contained messages in code. At first, no one had detected the secret communication. At least not until they'd noticed the one from their oldest brother Joe who'd referred to their childhood and the code games they'd played with each other.

From that hint, the messages had been easily deciphered. In truth her brothers had admitted they were fine and would remain on the planet with the women they'd met until it could be determined if it was safe for the women to go back through a time warp with them.

Piper hadn't believed it.

She still couldn't grasp the concept that they wanted to live here on a planet where their lives were in constant danger. And here she was bringing them the news that two of their sisters were missing or maybe even dead by now.

Blinking back the sudden bubble of tears, Piper squared her shoulders in defiance. Her sisters were not dead, and she would never consider them dead unless their bodies were found.

She was so deep in thought she barely noticed the strange noise behind her. Before she could so much as react, a large, hard hand clamped tightly over her mouth and a strong arm swung snugly around her waist. A split second later, she was swept off her feet and carried into a nearby clump of bushes.

Paralyzing fear gripped her as her assailant forced her belly down to the ground. His hand stayed tightly over her mouth, his other hand slid away from her waist. Suddenly a wall of pure muscle came down on her back, his heavy weight grinding her pubic bone and breasts painfully into the dirt.

God!

What was he doing? Was he going to rape her? Her heart picked up a frantic pace at the horrible thought, and she screamed into his hot hand.

The sound came out a dull muffle.

"Quiet! Danger!" a familiar man's voice sliced into her ear.

Jarod!

"The Death Valley Boys are coming," he hissed.

A shiver of dread zipped through her as she remembered the strange look that had passed between Jarod and Taylor last night. Remembered their warning that it was best she not meet them.

Suddenly she heard voices. Her eyes widened with surprise as not even a half-minute later five men walked into view.

Four of them carried a wooden litter. On it lay a stiff-looking corpse.

She could barely make out a bloodied wound in the area of the dead man's heart as the men started past their hiding place.

It could be a bullet wound or maybe a knife wound, she couldn't be sure.

All of the men including the dead one were naked, their varying sizes of semi-erect cocks dangling between their legs.

Great.

Just freaking great.

If Jarod hadn't come along when he had, there was no telling what would have happened to her if these men had seen her.

Piper swallowed against Jarod's hand as she watched the last man, a black-haired fellow around her age, the tallest of the group, leading a barefoot woman with tangles of shoulder-length red hair by a black leather leash hooked to a thick, most uncomfortable-looking collar around her neck.

Despite her total nakedness, the woman strolled proudly behind the men. She possessed no apparent shame. Acted as if she was fully clothed—her shoulders thrust back allowing her perky breasts to stand out notably. Despite the way she held herself, her eyes remained downcast as if she was a slave.

The small group stopped in front of an empty scaffold not more than twenty feet away from where Jarod and Piper hid in the bushes.

Grunting, the men hoisted the stiff body and the litter onto the scaffold, then stood silent while the tall, black-haired man led the submissive woman to the foot end of the scaffold.

"The dead one was their leader. The black-haired one is Blackie," Jarod explained. "He is most likely the new leader or the best choice for one, because he now has hold of the leader's woman's leash."

Piper watched as Blackie instructed the woman to sit cross-legged on the ground, facing the dead man on the litter. Her head was bowed, her hands in her lap.

"You must remain silent. No matter what happens. Do you understand?" he whispered to her in a voice so low she could barely hear him.

She nodded, and slowly ever so slowly, Jarod moved his hand from her mouth.

Before she could ask him what the hell was going on, the black-haired man began to wail.

The other men quickly joined in with a forlorn keening that chilled her to the bone and pierced her ears. She wished she could bury her head beneath her arms so she wouldn't have to listen to their screeching, or smell the gut-wrenching scent of death, but by the way Jarod's muscles were tensed up against her body she knew instinctively she dared not make a move.

It seemed like hours went by as the men continued to shout and chant. The hot sun beat down mercilessly against the barren ground all around her, and the intense heat from Jarod's body covering hers made her wish for a gallon of water to soothe her dry mouth, or better yet, an ice-cold swimming pool she could dive into.

Despite her growing discomfort, she kept her gaze glued to the man named Blackie.

There was an arrogant confidence about him as he stood there with his eyes closed and his head bowed, his long mane of midnight black hair spilling down to the middle of his back. She noticed the raised scars of old whip marks that crisscrossed his lower back and over his tight ass cheeks. He was also quite well-hung, his cock growing harder and thicker the more he chanted. The other men's cocks were hardening, too, and she wondered if maybe there was something sexual about those chants.

Again, she wondered what kind of society this was when it seemed all of the men she'd seen were scarred and didn't trust women.

Finally, the racket stopped and Piper heaved a sigh of relief. Her relief was short-lived when Jarod's hand once again covered her mouth. Before she could comprehend why, Blackie walked to the seated red-haired woman. Gesturing her to turn around and lie down, she automatically did as he asked, curled her knees upward and spread her legs wide, her hands covering her breasts as she began to pluck and pinch her large, red nipples.

Oh, my goodness!

"Her name is Jasmine," Jarod whispered softly. "She was a Queen of Queens, one of five and of the highest order. A High Queen who helped to make and change the laws governing all the Queens, the women and all slaves. She was accused of treason a couple of years ago. As punishment, she was sold to the Breeders who in turn trained her to become a sex slave. She was later sold to the Death Valley Boys. Now she lives purely to pleasure males."

Piper couldn't believe it. A queen turned into a sex slave? That would certainly explain the proud way she'd walked despite being collared and on a leash.

Piper's face flamed as Blackie, his engorged cock fully erect, kneeled down between Jasmine's legs, his body lowering over hers, his mouth descending upon her breasts like a seductive lover, suckling each of her nipples slowly into his mouth, drawing each of them out with his teeth until they looked so swollen Piper could feel her own nipples responding, aching, wanting Jarod's mouth taking her into his hot mouth.

Jasmine wiggled on the ground beneath Blackie, her hands slicing through his long black hair pulling his head closer, pressing his face deeper into her swollen breasts.

Blackie broke her hold and moved over her belly, his luscious lips kissing her lightly, his long tongue laving her skin, moving over her mons and finally settling between her widespread thighs.

Piper's cunt flamed and clenched, and she could literally feel moisture pooling between her legs at the suckling sounds ripping through the air as Blackie feasted upon Jasmine's pussy. She remembered how Jarod's moist lips had wrapped around her labia, his sharp teeth nipping at her quivering flesh, his long hot tongue sliding into her drenched vagina while she'd lain helpless and naked on his bed.

Piper closed her eyes at the sound of the woman's aroused whimpers, and felt Jarod's cock swell against her ass.

Obviously, the sight of the coupling was reminding him of what he'd done to her and was turning him on.

Just as it was turning her on.

The woman named Jasmine whimpered a few more times then they quickly grew into sensual moans.

"By the way she's trembling, she most likely hasn't been vaginally penetrated in quite some time."

Piper's eyes snapped open at his whisper, just in time to see Blackie thrust his thick cock into Jasmine who screamed out her pleasure. Piper bit down on her bottom lip to keep herself from crying out her arousal at seeing the two naked bodies intertwined on the ground while several men watched.

"It is the ritual of the Death Valley Boys to take a woman before the grave of a fallen comrade," Jarod's strangled whisper wafted into her ear.

Jasmine's lusty cries pressed in all around Piper. Her vagina clenched frantically as she envisioned Jarod's hard thickness sliding deep into her.

Gosh, it was like watching some erotic movie or something. Men standing around with their cocks fully erect while they watched another have sex with a woman, a woman who didn't appear at all in distress.

Heart pumping, body fevered, Piper watched as Blackie's handsome face contorted in a sweet agony as he finally shouted his release.

Lifting himself from the woman, his cock totally spent, he ushered the next man between Jasmine's legs and then the next until all men had taken their turn. Finally, Jasmine's lusty cries ceased, as all the men were satisfied.

They pulled the weary woman to her feet, and walked away from the scaffold containing the dead man. She looked back a few times at the dead body, a sad expression on her face. It made Piper wonder if perhaps she'd fallen in love with her captor.

Finally, when the small group disappeared over a knoll, Jarod's body sagged upon hers in apparent relief.

For endless minutes, his aroused breath filtered through the silent, late-afternoon air, and when he withdrew his hand from her mouth and climbed off her, he immediately yanked her to her feet.

To her surprise, fury sparkled in his eye.

"You shouldn't have left the tree house alone!" he spat at her as if he was admonishing a child.

His irritation instantly put her on the defensive. Sorry, buddy, but she was no kid. She was a woman with a mind of her own who didn't appreciate getting yelled at or told what to do. If she'd wanted that she could have stayed on Earth with her ex-boyfriend.

Picking up the knapsack, she flung it over her back. "It's no skin off your ass where I go. Why should you care?"

"I don't care." He ripped the knapsack away from her. "We will return to the tree house."

"The hell we will. I'm going to find my brothers."

She was able to take only one step toward the graveyard before he grabbed her by the wrist and yanked her roughly after him as if she was a mere rag doll.

"You son of a bitch! Let me go!" she shouted at his broad back.

"I will let you go when it is safe to do so," he grumbled, as he pulled her clear out of the cemetery and into a nearby forest of pine trees.

When they entered the forest, a wonderful cool shade washed over her overheated body but it did little to diminish the fury raging through her.

"If you don't let me go, I'll scream bloody murder." A lot good that would do out here in the middle of nowhere.

"You scream and the Death Valley Boys will be fucking you by sundown."

"Let them! I wouldn't mind at all."

Her words made him halt; he dropped the knapsack and yanked her hard, making her crash against the length of his hard body. The full length of his engorged cock pressed intimately against her belly, and she couldn't stop the shivers of arousal slipping through her.

"Obviously, watching the Death Valley Boys fucking Jasmine has lit a dark fire into your cunt. Perhaps I should fuck the fire from you?" he breathed, his stare hot, intense.

"And what if I don't want you to?" she lied, excitement quickly dissolving her anger. "What will you do then? Turn me into a sexual slave like that queen, Jasmine?"

"I've had plenty of experience in the life of sex slaves. It would be very easy to train you into submitting to your sexual desires."

"Oh, really? How easy?"

Down, Piper, you're treading on thin ice with this guy.

His one-eyed gaze caressed her mouth, and she could literally feel her lips tremble in anticipation for his kiss.

"With a petite female like you, I could do whatever I wanted to you."

"Really? What for instance?"

Her breath caught as his large hands left her waist and slid up underneath the flimsy top she wore, skimming across her flesh leaving a trail of fire.

Intimately, his hands slid over each of her aching breasts.

Oh, boy, this guy's hands feel so good.

Visions sifted through her mind. Darkness and a man's silhouette standing between her widespread legs, he was gazing down at her, lust shining brightly in one eye. One hand wrapped around the root of his long, thick cock, the other hand stroking along the engorged length, a dot of pre-come glistening at the slit of his swollen cock head.

She could hear herself crying in the darkness, begging him to fuck her.

But he didn't. He just stared at her, stroking that luscious swollen cock of his. Instead of plunging his thick vibrating flesh deep into her pussy, he grabbed her ankles, pulling her further down the bed until her ass sat at the edge, his head lowering between her trembling legs, his long tongue quickly thrusting into her pussy, making her climax instantly.

Piper trembled at the flashback sex dream, or fever sex dream as Jarod called them. Her pussy quivered deliciously, and she wanted to beg him to make love to her like she'd done countless times in those dark dreams.

He was watching her curiously as his soft whisper broke into her thoughts.

"The Death Valley Boys pierce the nipples of their naughtiest women."

A low moan escaped her lips. She sucked in a breath as he roughly tweaked her nipples, sending electric flames of erotic heat shooting into her breasts. The sensations made her arch her back, pushing herself harder into his hands.

"You like this, don't you," he breathed, his eyes flared with heat. "You would like to have your nipples pierced. To have your breasts chained. To have yourself at a male's mercy, wouldn't you?"

His head lowered, and he licked the sensitive area behind her left earlobe sending shimmers of warmth zipping through her. "You enjoy that I could not stop myself from sucking out the poisoned sex cream from your delicious cunt, don't you? You enjoy that your teasing scent makes me lose my mind, and all I can think to do is ram my shaft deep into your juicy cunt."

Oh, God, yes. Take me!

She wanted him. Wanted him to quench the fire he'd stoked throughout her ever since she'd awakened with his hot mouth feasting upon her clit.

His tongue tenderly licked the edge of her earlobe until a spicy tremor shot down her neck.

Damn, it felt so good.

"You still haven't shown me how easy it is for me to submit to my desires," she breathed.

The adrenaline rush of seeing that red-haired woman being impaled by so many men had turned her on fire just as Jarod had said, and now that those fever sex dreams were starting to haunt her, she wanted Jarod to bring her satisfaction. Wanted him to douse the overwhelming energy raging inside her, and she needed to do it soon or she'd explode.

A low growl grumbled somewhere deep in his chest. At the sensual sound, Piper found her fists uncurling from her sides and her small hands reaching out, her palms splaying across the hard contours of his chest, her fingers tracing the welted scars, feeling the damp heat of his flesh, the excited pounding of his heartbeat.

"You women are all the same. Always want to be serviced," he exhaled harshly against her cheek. "Although you are the first one I'm truly going to enjoy fucking."

"So, you've had your fair share of women?" The curiosity of knowing how many women he'd shared his bed with nibbled at her.

He didn't answer, instead his soft mouth descended upon hers in such a blissful desperation she thought she'd died and gone to heaven. His hard tongue wasted no time in crashing past her lips and sliding between her teeth, clashing against her tongue. Instantly, the heated flush shooting through her increased to dangerous levels, making her throw caution out the window.

His hands slid from her breasts, his fingers traveling over the length of her belly, her abdomen, dipping beneath the flimsy thong where his fingernails scraped erotically against her pussy lips and alternately plucked and played with her labia until they felt swollen and burned for relief.

"The Death Valley Boys would pierce your labia with silver labial rings and hang heavy weights off them whenever they needed to punish you," he said, as he sucked tenderly on the trembling edge of her mouth. A finger slid against her slippery clit, making her moan as he rubbed it so sensuously her vagina clenched with pleasure.

"They'd outfit your clit with a gold ring and attach a chain to it. They'd lead you around by that chain in front of all the males. You'd be totally at their mercy. Totally powerless as a woman."

To hell with the Death Valley Boys. She'd rather be chained and at the mercy of Jarod's sexual desires.

His moist lips charred her flesh as he worked magnificent kisses downward across her collarbone. A delicate smell of soap floated from his fluffy black hair, a direct contrast to the sharp masculine scent of his sweat-dampened body.

"Oh, God!" she cried out, as a hot finger slid about and inside her cunt, massaging her G-spot making her knees weaken with lust. Frantically, she clasped her hands around his solid muscular biceps, holding onto him for dear life.

"They might even give you an anal ring like they gave Jasmine, if you're really disobedient like she was when she first arrived." His hot breath brushed erotically over her right breast. She could barely concentrate on his words as his hot tongue flicked out and speared her quivering nipple through the cloth of her top.

"How…how do you…know so much about these men, about Jasmine?" she whispered, trying to breathe through the magnificent excitement his touches did to her.

"Because I was one of them."

He was a Death Valley Boy?

She could barely comprehend his answer as he sucked her hardened nipple into his wet mouth, biting her nub gently until she cried out from the pleasure-pain. A second finger joined the one already impaling her vagina, and she could hear the sucking sounds as he plunged in and out of her.

"Oh, God! Jarod."

She wanted his steely cock sliding inside of her. Wanted his hips crashing against hers without mercy.

She let go of his arms and slipped her hands beneath the loincloth, frantically grabbing at his balls. They were rock-hard, encased with silky flesh in her palms. He groaned as she squeezed and explored the two swollen spheres.

"Perhaps I want to be your sex slave for a while," she whispered, as she un-cupped his balls, and wrapped her fingers around the silky, hard root of his cock. His fiery flesh felt like a thick metal spike in her hands, and she could literally feel the weave of veins throbbing against her palms. "Maybe I want to be fucked by a man I'm so sexually attracted to that I can't stand it."

Suddenly, Jarod drew away, his fingers slid out of her pussy in one quick exit leaving her feeling empty and quivering with loss. His heavy breath flooded the air. Dampness curled the edges of his black hair and his nostrils flared.

Obviously, he was pissed off again.

"We must return to the tree house," he said, wrapping his hands around her wrists, and tugging her away from his gorgeous cock and out of his loincloth.

She looked down just in time to get a wonderful peek at his thick, red, pulsing cock just before he covered it.

Oh, God!

The man ached for some heavy-duty sex.

Just as she was aching.

"What's the matter? You're afraid of a few dead bodies?" she said, avoiding his gaze as those breathtaking tremors continued to sift up her vagina. Frustration screamed through every inch of her. Frustration and anger at herself for falling prey so easily again to his heated touches.

"It is sacred land," he said, and gazed through the trees at the giant graveyard, acting as if nothing had ever happened between them.

Her anger soared.

"Sorry, bud, but ghosts don't scare me. I'm going straight through."

His head snapped around and he gazed daggers at her.

God, he looked so dangerously sexy. So deliciously dangerous. An angry muscle twitched in his jaw, and she wanted to run her tongue over it, wanted to feel it pulsing as he thrust his gorgeous cock into her pussy.

Piper sighed.

Unfortunately, she didn't have time to argue with the guy, or spend some time getting to know this man, she had two sisters to rescue and three brothers to find.

A new urgency pulled at her.

"I'm through arguing with you, Jarod. I'm going straight through this cemetery, and I'm going to find my brothers with or without your help."

He quickly moved in front of her, blocking her way.

Piper stamped her foot with frustration. "Come on! I mean, really. How dangerous can a freaking cemetery be?"

"The freshly dead are only brought to the outer edges. The ancient ones are further inside. The graveyard extends for many miles and surrounds the entire village of the Death Valley Boys. There are guards who will spot us if we go through."

"So we keep our eyes peeled for the guards. There's no way I'm going back. My brothers deserve to know their sisters are in trouble, and they'll be able to help Taylor."

"We will go around, even that is too dangerous." The determined set to his jaw made her realize there was no use arguing with him.

Well, at least he wasn't insisting they go back to the tree house anymore.

It was a huge victory.

Wait a minute. Maybe it wasn't such a big win after all.

"We? You're coming with me?"

He nodded, and took the knapsack from her. His other hand grabbed hers, his fingers tightly interweaving with her fingers.

"I know of a place to rest for the night. We must hurry before it gets dark," he said, and pulled her deeper into the forest.

Oh, shit!

Maybe it would have been a better idea if she'd agreed to go back to the tree house with him? At least then, she could have slept in a separate room and not under the same romantic sky.

Chapter Five

Jarod couldn't believe he'd kissed and explored the woman he'd sworn he wouldn't touch again.

He'd been overly primed from watching those Death Valley Boys taking their turns with the delicious Jasmine. And Piper had made him so angry by seemingly wanting to get caught by them that all he could think to do to her was tell her and show her just a little of what would happen if she became their prisoner as Jasmine had become.

Ever since he'd discovered Piper's feminine footprints in the dirt leading in the total opposite direction that Taylor had gone, he'd tried to stifle the paralyzing fear something terrible could happen to her.

Last night when Taylor had drawn the map in the dirt, he'd purposely not mentioned the graveyard or the surrounding village of the Death Valley Boys. Their time with the Boys was one thing Taylor and he never spoke about. Jarod knew his friend had suffered at their hands, mainly because Taylor hadn't joined the splinter group that had mutinied against Jarod when he'd led the Slave Uprising years ago.

Taylor had trusted him to protect them back then and Jarod had failed him.

And now he had a female who, by the way her fingers were tightly interwoven with his, seemed to trust him just as desperately as Taylor had once done. He would have to ensure her safety. Make sure the guards didn't see them as he quickly ushered them through the forest which, through occasional openings in the green foliage, gave them eerie glimpses of the large black birds and ugly gray vultures that screeched and picked happily at the decaying flesh of an occasional dead body lying on the scaffolds.

The cemetery had grown since he'd been last here. He wondered with the cruel leader of the Death Valley Boys being dead who would take over if Blackie wasn't picked. Blackie was good leader material, but he lacked the ruthlessness of Laird. He also wondered when someone new took over if things would change with the Boys. Would the killing stop? Could the Death Valley Boys now live in peace?

"These Death Valley Boys," Piper breathed harshly, as she struggled to keep pace with his long stride. "Exactly why are you so scared of them? I mean if you were one of them, wouldn't they be your friends or something?"

"Cath has put a death bounty on my head. I am sure they would not hesitate to collect on it by killing me and returning my body to her. Also, I am afraid for you. The things they do to women…" To his surprise, he couldn't even finish the sentence as visions of naked women tied to trees getting whipped daily, and many other atrocities zapped into his mind. Just the thought of what could happen to petite Piper brought an icy wave of chills cascading through him.

"You're worried about me?" Surprise was quite evident in her voice, and he looked down to see her delicate brows knitted together with confusion.

"If you are who you say you are, the Hero brothers would never forgive me if something happened to you."

"Oh." She sounded somewhat disappointed at his answer.

"Just as I would never forgive them if something happened to my twin who is in their care."

"Your twin?"

"Yes, Virgin, she is with the youngest Hero brother, Buck."

Piper nodded. "I have a twin, too. Her name is Kinley." By the pain quite evident in her voice, he knew instantly she was one of the missing women. He remembered she'd said Kayla was the jogger. Kayla was the one who'd joined the Breeders group so that meant Kinley had been the one in the struggle with the two males.

"Does she look like you?" he asked, suddenly wanting to know more about Piper.

"Yes, we look pretty much alike. She's a couple of inches taller, just a touch thinner. But our attitude toward life is very different. She's really outgoing and popular, and I'm the quiet one who prefers to stay at home. How about you and your twin?" she asked. "Do you two look alike?"

"We look similar. But our hair color is different. She is a yellow hair."

She looked momentarily puzzled then smiled prettily. "You mean she's a blonde. It figures, Buck always preferred blondes."

"And what about you?"

"What about me?"

"Do you prefer a male with yellow hair?"

She shook her head. "Hair color doesn't matter to me. I prefer a man who is kind and gentle, and totally in love with me for who I am."

Love? That was a magical word with the Hero brothers and the women they'd taken for themselves. He remembered Virgin saying a word to that effect to Piper's brother Buck when Jarod and Taylor visited their small village on occasion to learn more of his planet Merik's language from the women and other skills from the males. He recalled how when Virgin or the other women mentioned the love word, the males' eyes had sparkled with a strange glow of happiness. Wait a minute—there was more than one word... Jarod tried to think back.

I love you.

That's what they said to each other. Those were the magical words that had them in each other's arms and kissing tenderly.

Odd how those magical words made people feel happy.

Perhaps if he used those words on Piper, he would be able to push away her worry for her sisters? Perhaps he could make that special look glow in her eyes that he saw in the others' eyes?

He dared a quick glance at her. The sight of her flushed face, tangled dark-brown hair that cascaded down to the middle of her back, and the way her small breasts heaved deliciously against the cloth that barely covered her curves made him want to take her into his arms, cradle her protectively against his chest and never let her go. He'd felt that way ever since he'd found her in the swamp.

Every day as she'd lain on his bed, her lithe body undulating beneath his exploring hands and his eager mouth as she was ravished by the fever sex dreams, his protective instincts toward her had grown stronger along with other instincts, such as coupling with her forever and doing anything she asked of him including leading her directly to the Hero males.

At that thought, he almost stopped in his tracks. Aside from what she'd told him, he really had no proof her mission into The Outer Limits wasn't a ploy to make him think she really did know those Hero males. For all he knew she could be working with Cath.

He shivered at the thought of Cath and the painful things she'd done to him while he'd been locked away under her control inside the prison.

No, he couldn't say those magical words to her. Not until he was sure she was who she said she was, and even then, he couldn't say those words because she was a woman. Past experience had taught him women were never to be trusted.

"You're too quiet. What are you thinking?"

A light breeze picked that exact moment to wash her delicate female scent all around him.

I'm thinking of mounting you. Of making you throb with so much pleasure, you will never want to leave Merik...or me.

"I am thinking it is time to eat and drink, and find some place to sleep."

He felt her fingers tighten ever so slightly at his last word. He swallowed hard. Tonight he would find it extremely hard not to mount her in every way possible. Tonight he would find it difficult not to show her what a male sex slave of Merik can only dream of doing to a woman.

* * * * *

They'd eaten quickly, and now Piper could see Jarod watching her through the moonlit night. He had barely taken his eye off her. Had hardly said a word to her and every time he so much as flexed a gorgeous muscle her pulse faltered with excitement.

Those flashbacks she was having about him were increasing.

The liquid of heated desire was dripping between her legs.

No matter how hard she forced her thoughts away from the flashbacks about the shadowy figure stroking his cock while she'd lain on his bed whimpering and begging him to fuck her, they wouldn't stay away.

She could feel the familiar stirrings of lust beginning to grow again, and forced herself to gaze around at their surroundings in an effort to stall the lusty feelings from grabbing hold of her yet again.

He'd picked a most romantic spot for them to rest for the night. The ground beneath her consisted of soft, warm, dry moss. Their walls were rocks, which concealed them from any prying eyes that might be lurking around in the night, and their roof was a glowing sky full of what appeared to be similar to flickering white clouds dancing in the black sky. Back home, they called them the Northern Lights.

The light show was capped off with a full moon shining down on them like a spotlight.

Since their earlier kiss and exploring touches, the sexual tension had simmered between them while they'd traveled along the outskirts of the giant cemetery.

He'd spoken in hushed whispers to her, explaining that her brothers figured the skeletons had probably been here for many, many years, preserved by the sun's unusual lack of harmful ultraviolet rays and lack of continuous severe weather. They'd even speculated that perhaps some bones were from a previous civilization that had for some unknown reason left the area of the vastly unexplored Outer Limits.

Now as he sat near her, watching her intently as if she was his prey ready to be pounced on, Piper couldn't help but be curiously eager to know more about this sexy hunk and more about the Death Valley Boys, and why they'd been having sex with that queen in the dismal surroundings of a cemetery.

She swallowed at the excited dryness in her throat, and forced herself to ask her questions. "While you were living with those…Death Valley guys, did you…did you do what those men did? Take one woman between several of you?"

"Yes."

Her breath caught in her throat at his quick answer.

He was watching her carefully, the corners of his sensual mouth tipping upwards ever so lightly as if he found her question amusing.

"What is it exactly you wish to know?" he asked, his gaze grew more intense.

Have mercy, the man got to the point fast, didn't he?

"Tell me about these Death Valley Boys. Why did you think that queen hadn't been…vaginally penetrated for some time? Why did they do what they did to her in front of a dead man? I mean you mentioned it was a ritual…how did that come about?"

His lips curled upward cutting loose a breathtaking smile that literally curled her toes. "You are so curious for such a petite woman. I will tell you what I know. The Death Valley village is only a little over three years old. It was started by the males who were able to escape the Slave Uprising alive."

Slave Uprising? How interesting.

She noted how he'd visibly tensed, and realized he was venturing into what was obviously a very touchy subject.

"In Death Valley, the males are only allowed to fuck a woman anally unless they wish to breed her. It keeps the woman sexually on edge, keeps her wanting to be vaginally penetrated. She is more controllable that way. Fucking a woman vaginally in front of a fallen comrade was turned into a tradition to show the Goddess of Freedom that what she did to us males has now come back to haunt any captive woman in the severest form of revenge. It is to show the Goddess how sexually deprived a Death Valley woman can get without the services of a male, and how she becomes so eager to be vaginally penetrated she is willing to have it done to her even by numerous men and in front of dead bodies."

"Oh, my gosh, what did this Goddess do?"

"Centuries ago, she enslaved all males. It has been that way ever since."

Piper's heart lurched as she remembered her brother's message. Remembered that men were considered nothing more than slaves. What Jarod was saying only confirmed it.

"Who was she? She must have been very powerful to change a whole way of life."

"From what my twin taught me, the Goddess of Freedom came from out here somewhere in the vastly unexplored Outer Limits many hundreds of years ago. She did not agree with the ways of the males, who had enslaved all women. She led a successful revolt against them. Most males were killed. A few were imprisoned and used for breeding purposes. This eventually led to the use of specially designed fucking machines. Machines used to impregnate women who are sentenced to prison and to a number of babies depending upon the severity of their crime."

Fucking machines that impregnate women? Was this guy kidding her? The seriousness in his face made her realize he was telling her the truth.

"Women are sentenced to babies?" Instead of years? It was unbelievable.

He nodded. "It happened to my twin, Virgin. Because of me, she was accused of educating sex slaves. She was then imprisoned and sentenced to babies for the rest of her childbearing years."

"Why because of you?"

Jarod sighed heavily, and she could see guilt swooping in around him like a sweltering blanket.

"I was forced to lie. Forced into telling the governing Five Queens that my twin educated me and several other slaves."

"Why would they make you say something that wasn't true?"

"It was a partial truth. She only educated me. That in itself would have sent her to prison."

"I think you're being too hard on yourself. I think she did a wonderful job in educating you. You speak very well."

He didn't say anything but by the twinkle in his eye he seemed happy to hear her compliment.

"You said you were forced to lie about the others. Why would someone force you to lie?"

"Not someone. Cath."

Piper shivered at his suddenly steely voice. He sounded as if this Cath woman wasn't even human.

"She had me beaten, brainwashed with drugs until I was saying things she wanted me to say. She has caused much trouble. She has betrayed several queens. She has gotten them out of the way so she can rule the women herself. She is much worse than the Goddess of Freedom ever was because Cath wants every male dead or lobotomized. She's already started to lobotomize all the male babies so they won't be any trouble to women in the future. I do not want to think what will happen when she starts to lobotomize all the male sex slaves. One day, if I get a chance, I will kill her."

Piper trembled at his words, and instinctively she knew he spoke the truth. Whatever horrors he'd suffered at her hands had instilled a hatred that would only get worse in time.

"Whatever she did to you isn't worth murdering her over."

His breath caught and he stilled in the moon glow. A muscle flexed in his jaw. Realized a fresh brand of tension zipped through the air.

He stared at her. His one eye was unreadable but the rest of his body suggested she'd betrayed him by saying the wrong thing. For the first time since she'd known him, she recognized the tiniest tinge of fear slithering through her. Everything inside her stilled, making her wary.

He was a big man. Wide shoulders. Large hands that were clenched into frustrated fists.

Should she maybe be afraid of him?

They were all alone. He was a stranger. She knew nothing about him. He could do whatever he wanted to do to her and no one would ever know.

Her brothers certainly didn't have a clue she was here. Her sisters didn't know she was with Jarod. Even NASA hadn't been informed about this secret mission to Paradise.

NASA had made it perfectly clear that from her brothers' reports they would steer clear of this planet.

No one knew except for a handful of her brothers' astronaut friends on Earth. All of them had all been sworn to secrecy regarding this top secret mission. The last thing anyone wanted to do was alert the public that astronauts were missing. It wasn't good for morale or for future space exploration.

So everyone involved with this mission had been sworn to secrecy. To say nothing, no matter what happened to Piper and her sisters. It had been agreed that if they never returned from this planet, it was to be considered hostile and no one from Earth would come looking for them.

Now that she thought about it, it had been a very bad deal to make.

It wasn't until Jarod's gaze collided with hers, and she noticed the frustration and pain in his eye that she realized his anger wasn't directed toward her but at this woman Cath, the one who'd beaten and brainwashed him.

Concern ripped through her. "My God, what else did she do to you?" Her whispered words had escaped even before she'd thought them through.

"She held me as her personal sex slave for more than a year."

Piper felt every word hit her like a blow.

Personal sex slave. To do with him whatever she wanted. Did that include beatings? Sexual torture? That would explain all the scars on his body.

"She forced me to service her and the prison guards several times a week, sometimes several times a day. The forced servicing is not what angers me. Servicing females is what I was trained to do from as young as I can remember. It wasn't so bad. It was the torture I endured at Cath's hands. Endless days of agony. Whippings. Ball weights. Painful nipple clamping, cock rings that caused enormous discomfort."

A muscle in his jaw jumped wickedly. "Then I discovered she was beating my twin when she was in prison, while she was pregnant. For what she did to my twin alone, I cannot allow her to go unpunished. And now Cath is said to be lobotomizing the male babies."

Lobotomizing babies?

Her stomach clenched in agony. Her fists tightened in frustration.

It was insanity. Surely that woman could be stopped? Surely, she wasn't so evil to hurt little babies?

"And she is lobotomizing the males that the Death Valley Boys are capturing for her."

"They're working for Cath?"

He nodded. "Yes, it was the only way for the males to survive. There was an agreement made by the leader of the Death Valley Boys and Cath. Without it, she would have sent the hunting parties into The Outer Limits to try to locate us. She even threatened to send in the drones that would have disintegrated the village if they had found us. But since the agreement, peace has reigned between the Death Valley Boys and Cath and her women. I fear what will happen when news travels that their leader is dead."

"What...what was the agreement?"

Jarod exhaled slowly and frowned. "It was agreed that the Death Valley Boys would raid the numerous cities, villages and hubs and take the women's male slaves and hand them over to Cath who would in turn lobotomize them. In return, Cath would leave Death Valley village unharmed and the Death Valley Boys in peace."

Anxiety tightened in Piper's chest. "And you agreed to this?"

Jarod straightened and shook his head, looking toward the flickering Northern Lights in the sky.

"All who did not agree with the leader were to be handed over to Cath. Taylor and I escaped before this could happen to us. We have been hiding from the Death Valley Boys and from Cath and all women for almost two years. Cath is the Goddess of Evil. She is putting others through torment right now as I speak. She must be stopped."

"Why doesn't someone go to the law? I mean you must have some sort of judicial system if you have prisons."

He sighed heavily, his clenched fists loosened and his wide shoulders slumped in defeat.

"Cath owns the law now. Unfortunately, no matter how much I wish to kill her, she is too powerful to stop by one man's hand alone. She has guards surrounding her every day. I have tried to get to her on several occasions but it is impossible."

Now he looked downright miserable, and Piper reached out to touch his arm in comfort.

"Nothing is ever impossible. There is always a way if you look hard enough and I don't mean murder. If you murder her that would make you as evil as she is, and I know you could never live with yourself after doing something like that. You have to go through a justice system even if a new one has to be created."

"You speak too innocently to be from Merik. I almost believe you when you say you aren't on a mission on behalf of Cath."

Piper groaned with frustration. "I am telling you the truth. I am not working for this Cath woman. Exactly what do I have to do to get you to believe me?"

At her question his one-eyed gaze moved intimately over the length of her meager clothing as if undressing her inch-by-inch. She felt her nipples tighten into hard buds. Warm liquid of arousal pooled between her legs.

Oh, gosh, and the sex dream flashbacks were starting again, too.

Her heart began a wild pounding, and her throat suddenly went dry as he lifted his hand and threaded his fingers through her hair. Just like he'd done in those shadowy flashbacks. Having his fingers slide through her hair felt so good. So right.

"A woman sent by Cath wouldn't be as soft as you are. Nor would she be as desirable as you," he whispered huskily.

Have mercy—he was drawing closer to her. Close enough so she could feel the sensual heat from his magnificent body wash all around her, his sharp masculine scent made her feel heady.

The calloused pad of his thumb rubbed erotically against the small dip behind her earlobe, and Piper closed her eyes at the shimmering sensations the sensual touch created.

"A woman belonging to Cath wouldn't smell so intoxicating."

His fingers swept the hair off the back of her neck, and he dipped his head and kissed her there. The feel of his warm lips pressing upon her flesh made her pulse skip, made her whimper with want for more of his tingling touches.

"A woman sent by Cath wouldn't allow herself to be dominated by a male...in any way or under any circumstance. But a woman not sent by Cath would allow me to do whatever I wanted to do to her...sexually."

Oh—my—God!

She met his gaze as red-hot heat roared through her.

"So...try me," she found herself whispering.

Chapter Six

She didn't have the harshness that most women on Merik possessed toward males, Jarod thought as he intertwined his fingers with hers, ushering her to stand.

Perhaps it was that delicate innocence that drew him to her?

An innocence he craved.

A need for her to accept him as a free male, and not view him as a sex slave.

With her free hand, her soft fingertips gently brushed along his chest, leaving a streak of fire in its wake, and making him inhale at the wonderful explosions her feminine touch created.

"What exactly did you have in mind?" Her voice was a trembling whisper in the moonlit night as she looked up at him.

Sexual starvation sparkled in her eyes. It was the same way she'd looked at him when she'd been held captive by those fever sex dreams from drinking too much of the swamp water.

"You're having flashbacks," he whispered. "They are quite common."

He'd known those sex dreams would come back to haunt her. Had known the mounting scene with Jasmine and the Death Valley Boys would trigger their return.

Her eyes widened at his comment, and he noticed her cheeks darken in the moon glow.

It was rare to see a woman blush. He'd seen it only when he'd been given a virgin to service.

But Piper wasn't a virgin. His tongue had told him that news upon his first exploration into her pussy when he'd first started to suck the poisoned cream from her body. To his surprise, he'd been disappointed at her not being a virgin but not really surprised.

Most women on Merik were not virgins.

"The flashbacks are the side effects of the swamp water," he explained.

She inhaled sharply.

"They are sexual cravings, an intense need for the male who cured you to bring you to orgasm again and again."

He saw the smooth column of her neck move as she swallowed.

"Will these flashbacks ever go away?"

"Do you want them to?"

"No."

"Then they will not."

"What do you mean?"

"They will stay with you for as long as you wish them to stay, or they will go."

Her beautiful lips parted to ask him another question, but he could hold himself back no longer.

His mouth descended upon hers, crushing against her petal-soft lips. She responded eagerly as he'd known she would. The lust had been flashing in her eyes since they'd seen the Death Valley Boys fucking Jasmine, just as the lust had consumed both of them when they'd touched each other afterwards.

His eager tongue parted her lips. When he entered her hot mouth, new blazes cleaved through him, making him groan with wonder at these fantastic sensations.

Goddess!

He needed to mate with her hot flesh. Desired to rip the cloth from her body.

He needed her so much he could literally feel the anger toward women sifting away being replaced by something else, something sweet and innocent.

Nothing in his past as a sex slave had prepared him for these warm explosions humming through him. Nor had he ever experienced such an unbearable desire for a woman.

He pressed harder against her mouth. Heated blood sang through his veins at the sound of her sexy whimpers.

His hands smoothed over her silky shoulders, down her arms, feeling her soft, fevered skin.

Despite his desire to rip at her clothing, he resisted, making her body tremble with excitement and making her whimper in frustration at his slowness. He enjoyed teasing her, and he enjoyed the way she was teasing him. The way her hands whispered over his scars and blazed over his taut abdomen heading toward his rock-hard cock had him groaning into her mouth.

He touched her velvety breasts, feeling the way the soft mounds hardened with arousal. Relished the way her stiff nipples poked against his callused palms, and the frantic beat of her heart as it thumped against his fingers.

A rough shudder ripped through him when she cupped his rigid scrotum and held him in her palms.

His cock screamed with need.

His brain was screaming, too—yelling at him to stop this before it was too late. Stop this before his heart was so deeply involved he would have to give up his control to a woman yet again.

Deep down however he knew it was already too late. Each warm caress of her sweet breath against his face made him weaken. Made him forget his past, made him lose his need for revenge.

She must have sensed his turmoil, because she pulled ever so slightly away, her lips brushing against his with earnest. "What's wrong? I thought you said that you wanted me to prove that I'm not lying. That I would do whatever you want me to do to prove myself."

"Yes," he breathed, swallowing hard at the way her fingers were now fondling and squeezing his rigid balls.

His cock throbbed with the need for release.

"Then why are you so tense?"

He stalled for as long as he could before meeting her questioning gaze.

"I don't know what's happening," he admitted, nibbling on her chin, feeling her tremble against him. Feeling his cock pulse, as he pushed his hard erection against her lower abdomen.

Her cloth-covered flesh felt so hot against his rod that he almost exploded.

"What do you mean?"

He tried to keep his voice impassive, uncaring. It didn't work. When he next spoke, his voice dripped thick with emotion.

"I want to fuck you so bad, Piper. Only you. Never any other woman again."

He saw her eyes widen in surprise. He, too, was surprised for confessing such an unheard of thing to a woman.

Male sex slaves weren't supposed to want to fuck one woman. They weren't even supposed to have feelings for a woman.

Especially the way women had treated him all his life, with such brutality. Such cold contempt.

"You're afraid."

Despite not wanting to admit it, not wanting to show his emotions as he'd been trained to hold under control at all times, no matter what, he nodded.

"I am, too. I mean we don't even know each other. But we can take it slow."

Slow.

Yet, his mind raced.

How could he take it slow? He wanted to explore these unraveling feelings of lust coursing through him, but he couldn't trust her.

She was a woman. And what if she really was a woman sent from Cath? If the Hero brothers weren't involved, he would take her at her word. He would risk his heart. Would fuck her senseless.

But because of the vow he'd made to protect the educated Hero males at all costs, so they could educate other males, he needed to find out if she was telling him the truth.

Needed to know for sure…needed to test her.

Feminine fingers brushed along the sensitive flesh underneath his cock, unleashing harshly erotic sensations making him groan.

"We can talk afterwards," she breathed. "We can get to know each other then. But first, I need to extinguish this fire screaming through me. Please, Jarod..."

With each of her fevered touches, each of her whispered words, he felt his self-control slip away. He fought against the familiar panic beginning to burn inside him. Fought against the fear she would dominate him. Swallowed back the sinking feeling that he would once again become a sex slave...

New sensations were enveloping him as her head dipped and she planted hot kisses across the expanse of his chest. To his surprise, her wet tongue flicked out and laved along the raised welts of old scars that once had no feeling but that now seemed so alive and vibrating with arousal.

"Don't be frightened, Jarod. I would never hurt you," she whispered, and she sucked a taut nipple into her beautiful, hot mouth.

Nerve endings burst as her fingers clamped around his cock.

"Take me, Jarod."

He grimaced at her soft whisper. Winced at the words he'd heard spoken by so many other women as they'd demanded sex from him.

"Fuck me as a free man, Jarod."

A free man. Those words he'd never heard spoken by a woman before.

She thought him free.

He almost laughed out loud at the irony of the situation.

A free man didn't have demons that wrestled inside him. A free man wasn't enslaved by a ferocious lust for one woman.

Was he?

Yet, as he thought of the magic words of love spoken between the Hero brothers and the Merik women, it brought the sweetest agony pouring through him.

Realization was beginning to sink in.

He'd declared he would never fuck a woman again. If he went through with his test, his vow would be useless.

Yet, if he trusted her and he didn't test her, and he was wrong, he would be leading an enemy into the camp of the people he'd sworn to protect with his life.

He had to test her.

Only then could he be sure she could be trusted.

Only then could he be sure his heart was telling him the truth. That she was who she said she was.

"Come with me," he whispered, and tugged gently on her hand.

She followed easily. Unafraid and eager.

He led her to the far end of the gully. Led her to the lone tree that shone brightly beneath the flickering lights in the sky.

"Stay here," he instructed.

She cocked her head prettily. "What are you up to?"

His heart pounded violently against his chest as she gazed at him. Her eyes burned with such intensity he almost gave in. Almost lay down on the ground as a male sex slave on Merik was supposed to do to show a woman she was his superior.

That she could do whatever she wished with him.

He resisted his training. Resisted the urge to submit.

"Wait here," he said again. His voice was a strangled whisper, his cock a piece of hardened steel demanding to impale her luscious pussy.

She nodded, the lust and curiosity on her face increasing.

He left her there.

It took him only a few minutes to find the item he was looking for.

When he returned he was a little surprised that she'd actually listened to him. It was unheard of for a woman to do as a male said. Yet here she was, standing exactly where he'd left her. Standing beneath the lone tree, watching him with lust-filled eyes as he approached her.

A savage need sliced through him, a need to pleasure her, to put away any lingering doubts he had for her.

He picked up his pace.

Her eyes widened slightly as she spotted the item he carried. Thankfully, there was no fear there, only curiosity and excitement. If there had been fear, he would have known she wasn't who she claimed to be, for she would have known his intentions toward her. Would have known she wouldn't be able to hide the truth for much longer.

"Usually a guy brings me flowers after we've had sex, not before," she chuckled. "What are they? They look like orchids."

He lifted one of the aromatic blooms from the small bouquet he'd picked, and touched the tip of her nose with it, watching her carefully for any reaction.

Still there was no fear in her eyes. But she could still be acting.

She inhaled deeply, almost too deeply for it to be safe.

He pulled the bloom away quickly and grabbed her as she stumbled.

"Wow, that's some scent," she purred, and pressed her warm body against his. "You should bottle it. It makes me feel so good. You could make a fortune back on Earth."

He would have to ask her more about this Earth.

His twin had told him about the Hero brothers coming from a planet called Earth on one of his visits to their village.

But she hadn't said too much. Only that women and males were equals on that planet.

It was a concept Jarod still didn't understand.

She'd also told him that if the brothers could find out if it was safe for them to return to their planet, they were taking the women and children back home with them.

He would ask Piper more questions about this interesting planet, Earth.

Later.

First, he had other questions to ask.

"Your reaction is to the scent of the passionflower. It is sexually intoxicating. It can also be mixed with other ingredients and used as a sexual drug."

She frowned prettily, blinking away the blurred vision the scent temporarily created.

"You drugged me?"

"No, the overwhelming sexual effect you are currently experiencing only lasts a minute."

She giggled and avoided his gaze. "Oh, somehow I don't think I'll be losing this sexual feeling for you. Ever."

He grinned, heat rising inside him at her words. The passion scent was working already.

From what she was revealing so far, this was going to be more than an enjoyable test.

"The scent also has another unique effect," he breathed, as he gently pushed her back against the smooth bark of the tree, her breasts jiggling provocatively beneath the gauze top.

"What's that?"

"I will tell you later."

Jarod fought against the urge to take her now.

To take her hard and fast.

Slamming into her tight, little pussy while she was held captive between his hard body and the solid tree.

Instead, he cupped her pretty heart-shaped face in his hands, tunneling his fingers through her soft feathery hair, and gently kissed her delicious frown away. Her lips were warm, ultra-responsive. She whimpered into his mouth, and her hands slid up over his shoulders, her fingertips feeling like satin as she stroked the back of his neck.

"Can't you tell me now?" she whispered as she broke the kiss.

He clenched his teeth, stopping himself from telling her what that side effect was. She could still be playing with him. Making him believe she was innocent.

All women on Merik were educated about the various effects of the passionflower. They also knew what would happen to them if they merely inhaled the scent. If she were a woman sent here by Cath, she would know exactly why she shouldn't have smelled that flower.

Yes, she could be acting. Trying to make him think she was all sweet and innocent, making him believe that the test he'd decided upon wasn't necessary.

It was time to do what needed doing.

He would suffer any consequences afterwards when he told her the truth about the effects of the passionflower, that is, if she'd spoken the truth. He would tell her he hadn't been able to take the chance of her possibly lying and that she was actually here to kill the Hero brothers. If she really was a sister to the Heros, she would understand his precaution and deception, and forgive him.

Gently, he kissed the pulse in her warm temple. Licked the edges of her eyebrow.

He could smell the heat of her skin.

Sweet.

Perfect.

A craving to see all of her silky flesh once again exposed to him, as he'd seen her in his bed during her fever sex dreams, ripped through him with lightning speed.

"Lift up your arms," he instructed.

She did as he asked, and he lifted the filmy cloth over her head, sucking in a harsh breath at the sight of her swollen mounds.

His abdomen tightened as he cupped their silky heaviness into his hands. Rock-hard, dark nipples shone in the moonlight, and he brushed his calloused palms against the glass-hard peaks, knowing that the too gentle touch would be torture for her.

She shuddered against him, her hands now eagerly descending along the length of his back, sliding along his spine until she reached the ties of his loincloth.

His cock pressed tightly against the loincloth, his swollen testicles felt near to bursting, his sex throbbed with the need to be touched by her, pulsed with the desire to slide deep into her silky, slippery vagina.

He looked up, captivated by the glassy look in her eyes. The scented effect of the passionflower had taken a firm hold on her.

A momentary pang of guilt sliced through him. When he told her why he'd asked her to smell the passionflower, would she hate him for not believing her?

He couldn't think about that now. He had to trust she would understand why he was doing this to her. Had to trust the passionflower would bring out the truth.

There was only a narrow room for opportunity. It was time to begin the test.

"Where do you come from?" he asked, as her fingers played with the strings of his loincloth.

His cock strained painfully against the material.

Ached to spring free.

"Earth," she whispered shakily, her fingers trembling so hard from the effects of the passionflower she was having great difficulty with the loincloth strings.

He could barely hear her answer over the harsh sounds of her breathing.

"Are you working for Cath?"

She shook her head, her brown, tangled hair bouncing in denial.

He grinned. Relief sifted through him. No, it was more than relief. It was as if a heavy burden had been lifted from his entire being.

It was as if he was suddenly…free.

"Are you the sister to the Hero brothers?"

"Yes, please, Jarod… I want you to fuck me, now." Sexual frustration marred her face. Her fingers continued to fight with the ties at his sides.

He reached and felt the shakiness in her hands, felt the fevered heat of want.

He released the ties.

The loincloth fell away, delivering his thick solid erection into the mild night air.

He bucked and groaned as her hands slid around his shaft, her fingers hungrily exploring the length of him until his cock burned with such a carnal lust he almost forgot he was supposed to be the one in charge.

There were more questions to ask. More things he needed to know.

He squeezed her breasts, pushing the luscious mounds inward until her dark nipples moved closer together. Dipping his head, he licked at her nipples.

"Do you really have sexual feelings for me?"

She'd said she did, but with the passion scent now racing full tilt inside her, she would speak the truth.

"Yes," she hissed.

Yes! She'd said yes!

"I've wanted you since the moment I woke up with your head buried between my legs."

"Is it because of the fever sex dreams you had that you want me?"

She frowned, confusion twisting her lips.

"Maybe…a little…some of what I remember has to do with it."

Her hands slid off his waist and settled onto his hips pulling him against her. His cock rubbed erotically against the thin cloth of her thong.

He could feel the heat pulsing between her legs. Could feel the wetness of her arousal drenching the material.

"But there's something else," she continued, and sucked his disfigured nipple into her hot little mouth.

He groaned as sparks shot through his tender, marred flesh.

"I love the way you protect my brothers." She licked the hard bud, her soft tongue laving it. The lusty sensations just about drove him crazy.

"I love the way you look at me. Like you want to possess me. Like you want to devour me. Like you have feelings for me."

Feelings were an understatement.

Her hands were exploring his back, her fingertips sliding over the whip welts and excruciating stun baton burns he'd endured at the hands of Cath and her women. Piper's fingers felt so tender compared to the extreme harshness he'd experienced at Cath's hands, and it almost brought tears to his eye.

Wherever Piper touched his flesh, she left a trail of fire.

A very nice trail of fire.

As if her touch was healing his flesh. Exorcising the demons that had settled inside the welts and burns over the years.

She let go of his nipple and looked up at him again, fire blazing in her lusty green eyes.

"And I really love that sexy eye patch. It makes you look so deliciously dangerous. So knight in shining armorish."

She loved his eye patch? He looked deliciously dangerous?

"What does knight in shining armorish mean?"

She dotted featherlight kisses across the expanse of his chest before answering, "Actually it is knight in shining armor, and it means you are my rescuer. A gentle man who saves the life of a woman, a man who fights for her and protects her at all costs like you protected me from the Death Valley Boys."

Her words wrapped around him like a wonderful warm blanket. Pride roared through him at being her knight in shining armor, her rescuer.

Dipping his head, he drew a luscious nipple into his mouth.

She cried out.

He chewed on the tender flesh, tasting the sweet, hard bud. He felt it peaking harder and harder inside his mouth. Felt her body tense. Felt the pounding of her heart beating wildly against his tongue.

His cock jumped wildly in her hot little hands as her fingers stroked his engorged flesh. He groaned and almost ripped her thong from her, almost plunged into her.

"Do with me what you wish," she whispered.

A woman allowing him, a sex slave, to do with her whatever he wished? It was something unheard of for him.

Looking up, he saw her staring down at him, and barely managed to hold onto his self-control at the lusty, glassy sparkles in her eyes. She was still deep inside the passion scent she'd inhaled.

"I need you inside me, Jarod."

She was speaking the truth. She wanted him.

Her softly spoken words made him crash to his knees, groaning at the loss of her satiny fingers as she was forced to unleash his hard cock.

His hands slid along her rib cage to her waist, holding her there as he moved his head lower, kissing the silky texture of her belly, poking his tongue into deep concave of her belly button. Curling his fingers inside her waistband, he slowly pulled the thin thongs down over her luscious hips, revealing the silky texture of her abdomen.

He could smell the sweet scent of her cream drifting from between her legs.

It made him mad with desire.

So mad, he picked up his pace and quickly slid her thong down her silky thighs and off.

"Jarod, please hurry."

She spread her legs wide to him, her fingers sifting through his hair, pushing him closer toward her steaming cunt.

The moon glowed wonderfully against Piper, like a spotlight, illuminating her pussy lips as they hung swollen and dripping wet with her juices.

He could hear her harsh, desperate breaths split the night air. He drew closer.

She cried out as he drew a plump lip into his mouth. He sucked on the tender flesh, chewed gently, scraped his teeth over the silkiness, pulling it away from her body until she was gasping and panting.

He did the same to her other lip, brushing his tongue lightly over her burning flesh between her labia, then biting, nipping and suckling the smooth pussy lips.

Her hands clenched tighter around his head trying to push his face deeper into her succulent pussy. She arched her body against him as he twirled his tongue around her rock-hard clitoris.

Using long, hard strokes, he made love to her clit and captured the sweet woman cream gushing from her cunt.

Her legs trembled violently.

Sensing she would fall any second, his hands slid around to tighten around her soft ass cheeks. Using his head, he pressed against her abdomen, pushing her harder against the tree. Then his tongue tunneled fiercely into her soaking pussy.

"Oh, God!" she screamed.

Her entire body shuddered, her hips bucked, and he sensed her vaginal walls would clench around his tongue any second.

He backed off.

She whimpered in frustration.

He still needed more information. Needed to make sure she hadn't been here for weeks, perhaps longer, and trained by Cath in the meantime. And he wanted to know more about this planet Earth.

"You say you are from Earth."

"Yes," she hissed, her fingers sifting wonderfully through his hair.

"And males and women are equals on your planet?" The Hero brothers had shocked him with that tidbit upon his first visit to their village over a year ago.

"Where I come from, yes, we are."

He thrust his tongue against her glistening clit.

She moaned.

"You were warned it may not be safe to come to Merik; why did you risk your lives?"

"Please, Jarod. Please fuck me."

He almost did as she asked. His cock was near to bursting. His mind ready to spiral out of control, to succumb to the reckless need burning inside him, the need to fuck her until she cried and screamed with pleasure.

"I asked you a question," he ground out. He could barely talk—his breathing had become ragged and harsh.

"We had to come back to tell our brothers."

"What did you have to tell them?"

"That it is safe to go back home."

Safe.

He almost wished he hadn't asked the question. It was safe to return to where she'd come from, she would leave him. He wouldn't see her again.

"Will you go back, too?"

She hesitated.

Her eyes stared down at him. The glassy-eyed look of the passion scent was starting to fade.

"I...I don't know. It depends."

"On?"

"You. Us. If there might be something between us."

He swallowed at the dryness clogging up his throat.

"What do you mean?"

Her face flushed. "I want to get to know you some more."

He almost took her right then and there. Almost stood and slid his aching, hard cock into her hot core to show her how much he wanted to get to know her, too. To show her how much he wished to pleasure her.

"I have to tell them something else," she volunteered. "I'll tell you if you lick my pussy some more."

The passion scent was definitely wearing off. She was beginning to go back to her old determined self. Grinning he licked her wet slit with one long torturous slurp that had her gasping. He looked up to see her swollen breasts heaving with her every breath.

"We crashed."

"When? Where?"

"A few days ago. Somewhere in the swamp. The ship may be lost. It was crushed. Swallowed up by the swamp. Please, more. I need more."

Relief poured through him. She would stay on Merik with him. He could get to know her some more. He could pleasure her anytime he wished.

She cried out as his tongue laved up her quivering channel again, stroking her velvety vaginal walls, and sucking more of the sweet cream from her.

She tasted so good.

He didn't think he would ever be able to let her go free.

"How did you get past the disintegration layers? Did your brothers not warn you of the disintegration machines in the message they sent? That they would destroy your ship if you returned?"

His hands tightened around her waist, preventing her from thrusting her hips against him. Slowly, ever so slowly, he pressed into her again. She groaned erotically. The sexy sound speared into his heart, melting his stamina.

Then she said breathlessly, "We thought we had some pretty heavy-duty deflector shields...thought they could withstand those disintegration machines. Maybe we miscalculated somewhere. My twin said something about sabotage, but I didn't get a chance to ask her. The smoke was everywhere. We tried to keep the ship from crashing but there was a virus in the computer. We weren't able to counteract it. All we could do was pray we'd get out alive."

"And then you crashed into the swamp."

She nodded. Her hands were frantically pushing at his head, pushing him closer to her pussy again, urging him to continue with his tongue fucking.

He held fast.

"You did good, Piper. Thank you."

"You can thank me by sliding that deliciously large cock of yours inside me, Jarod."

"That can easily be arranged."

Chapter Seven

Piper could barely breathe.

She burned with heat and with a wonderful killing pleasure.

Perspiration covered her feverish skin as she watched Jarod get up from where he'd been feasting upon her pussy. His eye blazed with hunger as he moved closer to her. His shapely lips glistened in the moonlight with her arousal.

Her cunt clenched wildly as she awaited his next move. Clenched and begged to be filled with his heat.

She was paralyzed with lust.

Lost.

Lost inside the beautiful sexual sensations his heated touches had created. Lost in the lusty way his tongue had played with her labia, claimed her clit and tunneled inside her vagina. But somewhere deep in the back of her mind she was grateful that before leaving Earth she'd been given a shot against all known sexual diseases and NASA's top secret birth control shot that would last her for at least three years.

She could be sexually free! Free to enjoy everything he would do to her!

Now he stood in front of her in all his naked glory. His testicles hung huge and heavy. He held his cock by the root with his hand, his fingers teasingly stroking the enormous length.

In the moon glow, it looked magnificently large. Unbelievably swollen, the thick web of veins pulsing. The mushroom-shaped head bulging, pre-come glistening from the slit.

"I want to fuck you so bad," he whispered. His hand was rubbing at his engorged erection now.

She shivered at the intensity of passion in his voice. Shivered as he drew closer. Masculine heat shimmered all around her. He smelled so good. So strong. So sexy.

She was so aroused, so ready to accept him into her.

Ached to be filled by a heavy piece of flesh. Ached so much, she could just scream.

He never broke eye contact as he pressed his cock against her. The mushroom-shaped head pushed deliciously against her vaginal opening, making her cry out at the unbelievable thickness.

At the fiery heat.

At the promise of an impending impalement.

"I'm going to love you. Love you so much you'll never want another male."

Oh, God!

Her breasts heaved with her every breath. Her nipples scraped erotically against his raised scars as he moved his chest against her. The unevenness of his puckered flesh was a perfect abrasion against her aching nipples. Rubbing her hot little buds against him, she moaned at the sparkling sensations the seductive movements caused.

She cried out again as the tip of his mushroom-shaped head began to slide into her tight slit.

Suddenly his finger was there, too. Erotically massaging the swollen bundle of nerves of her clit, blowing fire through her pussy.

Hot.

Vibrant.

Scorching fire.

She could barely stand the thickness, the pressure of Jarod's cock as he slowly sliced into her pussy.

His fingers dug into the curves of her hips. He pressed her harder against the tree, the bark scraping erotically against her ass cheeks and back.

He kissed her eyelids, kissed her cheeks.

Kissed her lips.

And he stretched her cunt as he slid into her.

Slowly. So agonizingly slow.

His finger played with her clit, making her moan at the explosion of sultry sensations tingling through her.

Making her so wet.

He was rubbing her hard now. Massaging erotically. Pinching her labia. Sending shards of erotic sensations screaming through her.

His carnal touches were holding her entire body on the edge, holding her captive as his big, juicy cock tunneled into her. She grabbed his ass, feeling his strong muscles flex against her fingertips, as she desperately tried to pull him closer.

He remained steadfast.

"You are in a hurry?" he chuckled against her mouth, as he kissed her so gently she couldn't stop trembling at the tenderness he showed.

"I need you, Jarod."

"I have heard from the Hero brothers that good things come to those who wait."

She could hear the amusement in his voice. It pissed her off.

"Forget what they said, will you? Fuck me!"

She was desperate now. He was filling her so deliciously. She could feel every pulsing inch of him sinking deeper.

And deeper.

Oh, God! He was so huge!

"Is it not true?"

"This isn't the time," she ground out, as his cock throbbed inside her pussy, tunneled deeper, pulsed harder.

"I cannot think of a more appropriate time to make my point."

Frustration clawed at her. Her mind reeled. Why was he doing this to her? Tormenting her? Keeping her from getting what she wanted. From what she'd been craving ever since she'd first met him.

"Okay!" she hissed, as she pulled harder at his ass. "You've made your point!"

He chuckled against her lips. Rubbed his stubbled cheek against hers, sparking wonderful sensations. She hungered for more.

The clean scent of him slammed into her nostrils; her hot cunt spasmed at the scent of male.

"You are so beautiful, Piper Hero."

Having said that, he plunged his entire cock into her in one magnificent thrust that impaled her to the tree. Her mouth opened in a desperate gasp as he began to thrust hotly into her. Fire pulsed up her pussy as her cunt frantically sucked at his immense length.

Wanton kisses rained upon her face.

Piper was frantic now. Frantic to slip over the edge of bliss Jarod was keeping her from.

In one quick jump, she clamped her legs around his thrusting hips. He groaned erotically as she dug the soles of her sandals into his rock-hard ass. She in turn, cried out as his cock slid deeper into her that one final thick inch, his swollen balls slamming against her flesh.

Holding tight to his muscular shoulders, she relished the sensual explosions gripping her as he rammed her pussy mercilessly.

"Yes!" she cried. "Yes!"

The sucking sounds of his cock sliding in and out of her split the night air.

Flesh slapped against flesh.

Masculine groans intermingled with her cries.

She scratched at his shoulders, digging her nails deeper into his flesh, as he continued to fuck her. Fucked her so completely, she couldn't help but let go of her every fiber of control.

Her frenzied vagina clamped and spasmed around his throbbing love muscle.

In and out he slid.

Harder.

Sweetly hard.

His fingers dug deeper into her hips. His cock destroyed her.

She was drowning in the wonderful sensations. Her ass burned as he kept thrusting into her, the tree bark scraping her tender flesh. She tossed her head back, cried out, shrieked as the sensations pulsed and played, and teased her.

One after the other, the erotic convulsions screamed around her, the fullness of his rigid cock blasting through her like an inferno.

He was moaning erotically into her neck as he hammered his pulsing erection into her.

Faster and faster.

Until she felt the hot stream of his semen release deep inside her womb.

* * * * *

"Do you think anyone heard us last night?" Piper whispered, as Jarod held her hand tightly and helped her over a fallen tree as they continued to skirt around the endless cemetery.

"If someone had, I am sure they would have found us by now."

"I'm sorry. I should have been more quiet, but you…"

He smiled when she faltered over what to say.

"You can say it. You couldn't hold your pleasure inside. I know very well how to service a woman."

Her eyes widened at his bold comment. "You sure sound confident of your abilities."

"I was a sex slave, trained in the arts of pleasuring a woman. Do you wish for me to remind you?"

Desire swelled in him quickly as he awaited her answer.

Immediately he noticed the change in her, the tension uncoiling through her petite body as she gave him a steady look. Instinctively, he knew she was ready to confront him about last night.

"You'd like that wouldn't you? So you can bring me more of those sensuous-smelling flowers that made me lose control for a while there. You never did tell me what that other side effect was."

He'd been hoping she wouldn't mention those passionflowers, at least not until he had her safely delivered to the Hero brothers. He had no way of telling how she'd react to being deceived.

Instinct warned him she would be a very passionate woman in her anger. The other day's scene had proved it when she'd prodded him by insinuating she wouldn't mind being fucked by the Death Valley Boys.

Now was not the time for an argument. "I will tell you later."

He made a move to go forward when she suddenly grabbed him by the elbow, her fingers digging painfully into his flesh, making him stop cold. She gave him a stern look that made him realize she wanted an answer now.

"Why did you ask me all those questions last night? And why couldn't I resist telling you everything without even thinking about stopping myself? Some of that stuff was confidential. You weren't even supposed to know about the spaceship."

"I apologize for asking those questions. I was curious about you. I will never repeat anything you told me to anyone."

She nodded obviously satisfied with his answer. "So? What was the side effect? And how long will it last?"

"The side effect only lasted until your first orgasm."

"Oh…"

He didn't miss the pretty pink color sweep across her cheeks.

"If you are worried about becoming with child by me, the passion scent you inhaled kills all sperm entering a woman's body."

"Interesting birth control," she muttered.

"You sound displeased. I can make you pregnant if you wish." The thought of having a child with her sent an unexpected jolt of erotic pleasure racing through him. Not to mention blood pouring into his quickly engorging cock.

"I've got birth control that will last for quite a while, so you won't have to get upset about it just yet."

"Who said I was upset? I think making a child with you would be a most pleasant experience."

The pink blush on her cheeks deepened.

"Just tell me the side effect. I don't need any more surprises like those flashbacks," she said softly, avoiding his gaze.

"The passion scent forces you to tell the truth."

"That's it?"

Jarod started. "Yes. As I said, the effects dissolve after your first orgasm."

She inhaled a deep breath; her sexy breasts heaved and pushed against the filmy material of her top, making Jarod long to cup their softness into his palms.

"Kind of like a lie detector?"

"I do not understand that term," he admitted.

"Never mind. I get it. You didn't trust me enough to believe that I was telling you the truth about me being their sister; so you thought you'd get me to smell those flowers, get the truth out of me and then fuck me afterwards. If I'd been a liar you wouldn't have fucked me. Gee, thanks for the vote of confidence."

Hurt brewed in her green eyes.

It made him curse himself for deceiving her the way he had.

"I apologize. I had to keep the Hero brothers safe. Even if it meant betraying you."

"Well, now you know they are safe from me, don't you?" She threw him a watery smile and started walking again. Obviously, he'd hurt her. No surprise there.

"I wouldn't have fucked you if I'd had doubts about you."

"Well, that's greatly reassuring. Maybe the next time you decide I'm not telling you the truth, you can give me another dose of that scent and fuck the side effects away. Gee, remind me to never make you think I'm lying to you, will you?"

"You are mad."

"Darn tooting, I'm more than mad. I'm pissed off," she said.

Early morning sunshine peeked through the forest splashing against her petite body as she climbed over another fallen log. Today she'd changed her clothing and wore a jade green-colored tank top that illuminated her pretty green eyes. And she wore a matching thong that gave him a perfect view of her curvy ass. A luscious-looking ass he'd love to penetrate at his earliest convenience.

Jarod blew out an aroused breath.

"When I have sex with a man, I expect there to be a certain trust between us. If you wanted me to sniff onto those flowers, you should have told me it was a lie detector test. I would have taken it anyway."

Her stride was quickening now.

"I trust you now. But in order to protect the Hero brothers, I could not chance anything. They have knowledge that can help us males be free of women. They can help us to be equals."

She stopped abruptly, and he crashed into her petite frame almost bowling her over.

Quickly reaching out, he caught her, holding her close to him. Her eyes sparkled with anger and her body felt so deliciously warm. She even smelled faintly of last night's sex. Longing ripped through his loins, and he couldn't stop himself from lowering his mouth over hers and gently kissing her, teasing her lips until she opened up to him, allowing him to come inside. Allowing him to once again explore the dark, lush cavern of her mouth.

She tasted so shockingly sweet and innocent, and he groaned as he felt her vibrant curves melt against him. She was nothing like the endless streams of hard, cool women he'd been made to service over his years. She was unique. A woman he needed to keep in his life.

He kissed her deeper, savoring the silkiness of her rose petal-soft lips, forcing the anger from her tense body, forcing her to remember what they'd shared last night.

His cock convulsed and grew, pressing hard against her hot flesh until she swayed in his arms and whimpered.

The sexy sound almost overwhelmed his senses. Almost made him forget that while they were standing here, near the cemetery, they were in constant danger.

He needed to stop the delicious kiss now, before he lost total control and fucked her right here so close to danger. Last night had already been a very stupid thing to do—making her cry out her pleasure so many times. Now that he looked back on it, he was surprised they hadn't been discovered yet.

He needed to stop kissing her. Needed to get his bearings. They had to keep moving. They had to get away from here.

Yet, he couldn't release her when he finally broke the kiss.

"The first thing you need to do if you want a woman as your equal," she whispered, as her body trembled against him, "is to learn to trust her. Without trust in a relationship there is no foundation."

"I trust you now. I truly do. Please believe me."

She nodded, and the tips of her passion-swelled lips tilted into a beautiful smile.

"Good. I'm glad we understand each other."

Within a split second, her smile disintegrated and an icy rush of fear sliced into her green eyes. His heart lodged in his throat as intense pain sliced into his shoulder.

He'd been hit with something, something that took the very breath out of his lungs and left him unable to protect Piper.

Despite fighting to stay standing, his legs weakened.

His mind numbed.

"Run" was all he could say when he saw a shadowy figure sneak up on her. A male stood there. He raised his muscled arms showing Jarod a large branch. He watched in unbelievable horror as it came down, crashing over Piper's head.

Momentary pain racked her face, and then her eyes fluttered closed on a moan.

She slumped to the ground.

A moment later, he joined her.

* * * * *

When Piper came to, she had a splitting headache. It felt as if someone had hit her with a two-by-four.

"Son of a bitch!" she moaned, as she gingerly pressed her fingers to the painful goose egg at the top of her head. Her fingers came away streaked with warm blood.

Wincing, she struggled into a seated position, and fought the brief sensation of dizziness.

Where the hell was she?

She gazed around the room, which appeared to be eight-foot by eight-foot and maybe seven feet high. The ground beneath her was dirt and hard as a rock, not to mention cold. Her sparse clothing wasn't keeping her warm, that's for sure.

Her thoughts felt slow, sluggish and she tried to remember what had happened.

Come on! Think! she mentally screamed at herself, as she gazed at the walls, which appeared to be made out of animal skins patched together like some sort of antique quilt. In the middle of the room a small fire flickered, the gray smoke curling straight up toward a hole in a straw thatch ceiling.

Someone was lying beside the fire huddled beneath blankets. The feathery black hair was unmistakable.

"Jarod!" she squeaked, suddenly remembering the arrow protruding from his shoulder before she'd been hit from behind.

The bundle moved slightly, moaned then fell silent.

Oh, God!

She flew to his side, barely hearing the sound of chains echoing through the room.

Jarod looked absolutely awful.

Perspiration drenched his flushed face and he shivered. His one eye was open and glazed with pain. He was looking at her, but she knew he wasn't here with her, he was somewhere else. His next word confirmed her thought.

"Cath?" he whispered, in a strangled, frightened voice.

"It's me, Piper. You're going to be all right, Jarod." She felt his damp forehead. Goose bumps chased up her spine. He was burning up!

"Hey! Somebody! Get your ass in here!" she screamed. "I need a doctor!"

She stood and headed for the flap, which she perceived was the doorway, when something hard strangled around her neck, stopping her cold.

That's when she felt the cold metal of a collar around her neck. A chain dangled down her back and headed toward a metal hoop protruding from the ground in the far corner.

There was an odd-looking padlock on the hoop.

Oh, great! Just freaking great!

They'd tied her down like she was a dog.

Muffled voices bounced around outside the shelter and she wondered if maybe it hadn't been such a good idea to call out to her captors.

She found her way back to Jarod who still stared unseeing at her. She needed to get a look at the shoulder wound. Needed to see how bad this was.

Gulping against the dry knot of fear clogging up her throat, Piper whipped aside the blankets covering Jarod's chest.

To her surprise, she discovered he'd been patched up with clean, white bandages that were wrapped snugly around his chest and shoulder. It looked like a professional enough job.

Suddenly the door flap whipped aside.

A man entered.

Not just any man.

Blackie.

Gosh, he was a big fellow. A lot bigger this close-up than he'd been out there in the cemetery.

When he spotted her crouched over Jarod, he smiled, but it was a cool smile that sent shivers racing up and down her spine.

"So, we meet again," he said as he strolled into the shelter.

"I wouldn't call our first meeting very proper since you didn't introduce yourself before you knocked me out, Mister Blackie."

His dark eyes narrowed in the firelight. "You know my name?"

Oops.

He cast a glance at Jarod who lay as still as a corpse. "He told you?"

"Forget the freaking introductions, okay? Jarod needs a doctor. You better get him in here, pronto, or I'm going to take this chain and wrap it around your scrawny neck 'til your eyes bug out."

For effect, she stood and grabbed a length of the chain keeping her hostage between both hands and pulled hard.

His eyebrows lifted with amusement. "I told my dead brother you would be a handful when we first started tracking you."

What the hell was he talking about?

"I told him to be very careful of your beauty. Told him a woman as stunning as you can be distracting, hence lethal. Unfortunately, he didn't listen to me. I must compliment you on killing him so quickly. One plunge of his own knife directly into his heart. If I hadn't seen it with my own eyes, I wouldn't have believed it."

"Listen, buster. You've gotten me mistaken with somebody else. Okay. Just cut this crap and get a doctor for Jarod. He's burning up with fever."

He frowned, and stared at her thoughtfully. "Such unusual concern for a male. Why?"

Forcing herself to steady her breathing, she remembered that women were the superior race on this planet.

"Never mind. Just get the doctor in here."

"No need. His fever will leave shortly. He's been given a quick healing injection already. It was most unfortunate he was injured. The men didn't recognize him. They only saw you and did not want the same fate as their leader, and so you both had to be put out of commission quickly."

He took a step toward her.

A surge of fear skipped into her veins and her grip around the chain tightened. "I'm warning you. You take another step closer and you'll regret it."

"I already regret not fucking you the instant I captured you last time. You have a wild streak inside you that needs to be tamed by a male."

"I told you that you've got the wrong…"

Realization slammed into her like a sucker punch.

Oh, shit! Was he talking about her twin sister, Kinley? Had the Death Valley Boys attacked her sister?

Okay, she could handle this. Think! Girl! Think! If she gave this guy the impression she wasn't Kinley then they would go after her.

"You hit me a little too hard on the head. Refresh my memory, will you? Exactly what happened to me when I was last captured?"

"You are still playing that game, are you?"

"What game?"

He chuckled and took another step toward her.

She backed up and readied the chain in her hands. How she was going to do any damage to this big guy was beyond her, but she wasn't going to allow him to so much as touch her.

"Pretending you don't know this is Death Valley Boy territory, and the fact that any woman who ventures onto our land belongs to us."

Oh, boy.

"Therefore you now belong to the Death Valley Boys. The males haven't taken too kindly to having their leader being killed by a female. I'm finding it difficult to keep them from wanting to punish you, my dangerous warrior woman. Perhaps I can persuade them to go easier on you. Perhaps you'll allow me to run my tongue along that scar on your belly as you allowed me to do the last time we met?"

Of course, Kinley's appendicitis scar.

He'd gotten that close to her sister? She wished she could question him as to how her sister was doing and where he'd last seen her, but she'd give herself away and they'd go after Kinley.

This was just great. Her sister had murdered some guy, which the guy probably deserved, and they thought she was the one who had done it.

Time for a plan, girl.

No plan came to mind.

His eyes darkened with lust. "Not many women allow themselves a scar. They get rid of it with the injection. Why you didn't get rid of yours isn't my concern. Rest assured, though, it makes you look so sexy. How about giving me another peek at it? So I can taste it again."

"I don't think so. Not after what happened during our last encounter." She was fishing for more information, and that question seemed safe enough to ask, considering he'd obviously watched his leader getting killed by Kinley. Thankfully, he took the bait.

A frown tugged at his handsome face. "You appeared to enjoy what I was doing to you…that is, until the leader showed up and decided he wanted you for himself. Too bad you killed him before either of us could have a taste of your pent-up passion."

Piper sighed her relief. It seemed as if these men hadn't physically hurt Kinley. She'd been able to fight them off and escape.

"Come closer to the fire; let me see that sexy scar again."

Thankfully it was dark enough in here that he couldn't see she wasn't wearing a sexy scar. On the other hand, what she was wearing would reveal to him that she didn't have a scar the minute they hit sunlight. And what was he saying about letting him taste her scar again? Exactly what had Kinley been doing with Blackie?

Cripes, that girl drew men to her like a moth to a flame.

"You can't touch me. I belong to Jarod."

Blackie licked his bottom lip as he looked over at Jarod's prone figure.

"I am an ex-sex slave just like Jarod. I can bring you so much joy. Perhaps more than Jarod has done."

Arrogant son of bitch.

Her grip on the chain tightened. "You think highly of yourself, don't you, Mr. Blackie?"

"I know what I want, and I want you under me before the other men get a chance. Once you have a taste of my charms, the others will seem like inexperienced boys, and you'll keep coming back to me over and over again."

"Sorry; like I said, I belong to him. So why don't you just let us go?"

He growled in frustration and turned to leave, then stopped at the door. "You will stay here with Jarod. And you will rest so that you will be ready for the punishment from the Death Valley Boys. Payment for what you have done to their leader. And I will be the first to take that payment."

Having said that, he turned and left.

Shit! She was in a heap of bad trouble, and it didn't look as if she was going to get out of it any time soon.

Chapter Eight

Fire burned Jarod. It seeped through his limbs. Devoured his body until he could barely stand it.

The walls in the dungeons of the prison were rock.

Ice-cold rock.

He couldn't remember how long he'd been chained here in the darkness. But by the pain roaring through his weight-drenched balls it had been quite some time. The coolness of the rock nestled against his back did little to douse the lines of fire roaring across his flesh from his most recent whipping.

Feminine hands roughly groped his heated flesh. Slapped his penis. Yanked on his weight-laden balls until he screamed in pain, and jerked fruitlessly at the chains around his wrists and ankles.

Her disembodied voice echoed eerily through the darkness. "You dare to lead a rebellion against women? You will be taught a lesson you shall not soon forget, my sex slave."

A couple of strong hands slid under his chin and held his head captive. Fingers pried his right eye open, keeping his eyelid from closing.

A long knife gleamed in the firelight of a torch as it drew closer and closer.

Bile rose up in his throat as he realized their intentions.

Searing pain unlike anything he'd ever experienced before ripped through his eye.

He screamed.

And screamed.

He awoke on a gurgled cry.

"Oh, thank God, you're awake."

Piper's voice?

Despite the grogginess pulling him back under, he forced himself to open his eye and blinked at the concern flushing her pale face.

He tried to move, to reassure her everything was fine, but a devilish pain lanced through his shoulder, shot into his chest and seared up into his neck, stopping him cold.

"Don't move," she whispered, her warm fingers curled around his chest hairs, urging him to remain still.

He forced the grogginess away. He didn't have too much trouble doing it. He'd had years of experience of staying alert despite his injuries.

"What happened?"

"They shot you in the shoulder with an arrow. You had a high fever. It's almost gone now. They said they gave you something called a quick healing injection. Your wound is already half-healed. It's amazing the technology these people have access to."

He peered around at the surroundings. His gut clenched horribly the instant he recognized the hide house belonging to Blackie.

Oh, Goddess of Freedom! His worst fear had come true. The Death Valley Boys had captured Piper.

"You must leave." His mouth felt so dry he could barely talk. He needed some water, but first he needed her out of here. "Leave now. Cut a...hole in the back of the hide house and leave. Don't look...back."

"I can't."

A cold wave of fear splashed over him. Maybe she didn't want to leave? Maybe they'd already done things to her? The Death Valley Boys were notorious for finding a woman's sexual weakness and using it to their advantage. And from his experience with Piper, she was a highly sensual woman.

She enjoyed sex, most likely all kinds of sex.

That would be her downfall.

"Have they done anything to you?" He held his breath awaiting her answer.

"Aside from a nasty headache from the wallop on my head, they've been rather sociable."

Sociable?

That was not a good sign. If they were being nice to her it only meant they were still trying to decide what role she would play for the Death Valley Boys.

She moved a little closer. His blood ran cold at the sight of the black metal collar wrapped around her neck. A chain hung from the collar to where it was locked onto a hook in the ground.

"I tried to break free, but it doesn't budge," she said.

Jarod cursed, and once again tried to move, but the pain kept him still.

"I need to…get you out of here."

"Please, don't move. I know it's healing really fast, but I don't want you to reopen it."

"I don't care…about the wound."

If he could somehow rip the stake out of the ground, he might be able save her.

At that instant, the flap opened and his worst nightmare crawled inside.

"Glad to see you are awake, old friend," Blackie said as he entered. He quickly gazed at Piper and smiled. "And we thank you for the delicious present you brought for the Boys."

"She is not a present for you."

Blackie's eyes darkened dangerously, but Jarod wasn't afraid. He would kill Blackie, or any male who dared touch her.

"Are you saying she belongs to you?"

Jarod's head snapped up and he found Piper staring at him, her eyes pleading with him.

"She is mine."

"Are you prepared to speak to the council, Jarod? Are you prepared to explain why you were on the outskirts of the cemetery? Why your woman killed Laird?"

"She didn't—"

"Jarod knows me so well." Piper broke in—preventing him from telling Blackie she didn't kill anybody. "He knows I don't like to be forced into anything. I had to kill the leader because I didn't belong to him. I belong to Jarod."

"It is true," he agreed, wondering why in the world he was going along with her story. Whatever her reasons, it wouldn't do to argue with her in front of Blackie. "I have captured her and turned her into my sex slave."

He noticed Piper eyes widen slightly at what he'd said, but he also noticed her shoulders slump in relief.

Blackie was watching him carefully. His old friend had always known Jarod hated women because of how they'd kept males enslaved. Blackie had understood what Jarod had wanted to accomplish with the Slave Uprising.

He'd wanted the male sex slaves to reach a new alliance with the women. To be treated better. To have the whippings stopped among many other things.

Blackie had not been one of the many who had mutinied against him during the Uprising, but after he'd escaped the Brothel Town, he had joined the Death Valley Boys, the same males who had betrayed Jarod and then raped and pillaged the women of Brothel Town. He'd also remained behind in Death Valley even when Taylor and Jarod had begged him to leave with them after discovering the Boys were allying themselves with Cath, the woman who had caused so much grief for his sister Virgin and himself, and countless others.

"I don't have to explain anything to you or to the council, Blackie. I no longer belong to the Death Valley Boys."

"You best spill your guts to the council or at the very least they will kill you, and order the males to give Piper a good punishment for killing our leader. There is talk about it already."

Horror raced up Jarod's spine as Blackie's hand flew to the lock at Piper's collar.

"Keep your grubby hands off me, mister!" Piper spat, despite the fear that flashed in her eyes.

He knew without a doubt she'd start fighting any second.

"So much fire," Blackie grinned, as he easily clasped her two wrists together in the palm of his one large hand. "I will enjoy fucking you, my warrior woman."

Jarod swore when Blackie's hand cupped Piper's breast.

"Do not touch her! She is my woman, Blackie. I challenge you!"

Blackie froze.

Piper reacted instantly and slammed her palm up under his chin.

Growling in pain, Blackie automatically let her go. Piper grabbed her chain in both hands, yanked them between her hands and held it up. Anger sparked in her eyes.

"So help me God, if you touch me again, I will wrap this around your neck and choke you to death," she screamed at him.

Blackie smiled.

"Such fire in your warrior woman. Jarod, I accept your challenge."

"Dammit Blackie! If you touch her—"

"She won't be harmed. We still honor challenges in Death Valley."

He produced a key and warily watched Piper as he slid it into the lock that held the chain to the loop. The instant the lock clicked open, Piper made a dash for the open flap.

Jarod urged her on.

But Piper was no match for the muscular Blackie. Quickly grabbing her by the waist, he swung her back inside as if she was a mere puppet.

He grinned widely as he pulled her close to his tall frame and gazed down at Jarod, his dark brown, almost black, eyes smoldered with lusty anger.

"When you are feeling better, you will be taken to the council. In the meantime, she will be prepared for what happens after the challenge."

Before Jarod could protest again, Blackie hauled Piper out of the hide house.

* * * * *

Furious with the man called Blackie, Piper kicked at his shins with her feet as hard as she could.

To her surprise, he didn't even flinch.

"Quit manhandling me, you rude son of a bitch!"

Men, most of them naked, watched hungrily as Blackie pulled her down the night-darkened streets. The men whistled and catcalled. Thankfully, none made a move to touch her.

The brute hauled her into a large hide house. Inside, it was warm and smoky, and dimly lit by candles flickering in various sconces set about the room's walls. A beautiful blonde-haired woman stood quickly from a smoldering fire pit where she'd been stirring something in a cast iron pot. She looked to be around Piper's age. She was very tall with pretty blue eyes. Her hair parted to the side, straight and long, all the way down to her waist.

And she was naked.

What else was new around here?

Her body was very well-muscled and toned with an hourglass figure Piper would absolutely die for along with very large breasts and a shaven pussy.

"Gemile, prepare her," Blackie shouted at the woman.

Piper could tell Blackie was angry. Could feel the tenseness in his rock-hard body as he'd held her close to him while he'd spoken to Jarod. Obviously, Jarod's challenge had him worried.

Very worried.

Without warning, he grabbed her by the chin and held her head steady as he whispered coldly, "You do as they tell you or they will be punished. And you right along with them."

He let her go and handed her chain to the woman. Piper was about to tell him exactly where he could go with his stupid punishment when he turned and stomped out without a backward glance.

"Charming fellow, isn't he?" Piper grumbled, as Gemile yanked on her chain and led Piper through another door.

She gasped in shock.

Cages lined one of the walls. To her horror, some of them contained women.

Naked women, all of them quite beautiful and well-toned. They sat hunched quietly in their individual cages and watched warily as Piper was paraded past them.

She was pushed through yet another open doorway into a smaller room.

Before she knew what was happening another woman, a very tall brunette with two odd-looking chignons plopped on each side of her head making her look like Princess Leia in the old classic *Star Wars* movie, grabbed her by her wrists and led her over to a rather large, wooden steaming bathtub set in the middle of the room.

"Women do not wear clothing in Death Valley. These clothing must be off your body. We will strip you down," Gemile said quietly.

"Like hell!"

"She appears frightened," the other one holding her wrists said. This woman was also beautiful, with pretty brown eyes, a dusting of freckles over her nose and a cute cupid's arrow mouth. She was tall and just as toned as Gemile.

And just as naked.

Good grief, it must be nice to feel so free with one's sexuality as these two appeared to be.

"Who says I'm scared?" she said defiantly.

She was scared, just a little. Ticked off was more like it, though. It wasn't every day she was led around by a chain and collar as if she was a slave. She could put up with a lot of stuff, but giving up her independence wasn't one of them.

"Hold tight to her, Lena. She appears to not want to be here."

Gemile made a move to tug down Piper's flimsy thong, when she stepped on the woman's toes. Hard enough to get her to yelp in pain.

"Lay a hand on me and you both die."

Gemile frowned, and darned if she didn't have tears brewing in her eyes.

"Please do not make this difficult for us. Blackie said I must prepare you. This means a bath. Please do participate, or we will all be whipped." The sincerity in the blonde's voice made Piper roll her eyes and feel like a heel.

Blackie had warned her she better do as they said. The last thing she needed was for them to call him in here, and for him to realize she wasn't wearing that sexy scar he'd seen on Kinley.

"Fine, strip me, then."

They moved quickly and efficiently. Within a minute, she stood before them totally nude.

God! Was this embarrassing or what?

They said nothing as the two of them ushered her into the tub.

The tub was filled almost to the rim and the water was ultra-warm, floating full of lilac-smelling bubbles.

Pushing her into a seated position they proceeded to bathe her.

Intimately, she might add.

Using soap that smelled the same as the lilac bubbles, they washed her hair and ran their hands all over her body, including her breasts.

Cleaning her thoroughly from behind her ears right down to the tips of her toes. When they made her stand and she thought they were finished, they attacked the area between her legs.

Their fingers caressed her pussy, sliding erotically against her clit, sinking into her vagina, and rubbing her labia so sensually, Piper had to bite her bottom lip to keep from moaning and giving away her enjoyment. She was still a little sore from Jarod's hard plunges from when he'd made love to her last night, and the rawness of it along with these women's gentle touches was turning her on hotter than a freaking furnace.

But when a finger slid into her anus, Piper figured it was time to protest.

"If you want to keep that finger, you will remove it right now," she barked.

Giggles erupted from the two women.

"You will learn to appreciate a finger there and elsewhere," Lena said coolly.

"The hell I will," Piper answered, and tried to squirm away.

But Lena held her firm, pushing hard at the back of her head forcing her to bend over.

"Come on! This is ridiculous."

"Keep calm, newcomer." Gemile spat. "Or the finger will hurt and so will the rest of us if I cannot deliver a favorable report to Blackie."

Piper swore softly as the delicate finger intruded into her ass again. Gemile's gentle prodding made her breath catch as erotic sensations produced an odd pleasure-pain. She probably would have enjoyed it a heck of a lot more if she was at ease with sex like her sisters Kayla and Kinley were.

"Is she an anal virgin, Gemile?"

"Yes," came Gemile's reply. "Very tight indeed. Apparently, Jarod has not taken her there."

Damn bitches! Piper's face flamed as the woman's finger finally left her.

"The Death Valley Boys will be pleased. Perhaps they will leave us alone for a little while," Lena muttered.

"I don't want to be left alone," Gemile replied. "I enjoy having sex with them, even if it is only anal most of the time."

"That's because the Breeders trained you so well, that's all you are good for," Lena chuckled.

"What the hell is this place anyway? What's with the cages?" Piper asked, as she was led out of the tub and they began to towel-dry her.

"Surely you must know. This is Death Valley. It is where the sex slaves have hidden since the Slave Uprising over three years ago. These cages are where we women are housed when we aren't required. It is the exact opposite of our world where we ruled. Here the males rule."

Lena let go of her, and with a fluffy towel, Gemile attacked Piper's breasts with such vigor she couldn't help but respond. She could literally feel her nipples elongating, swelling and aching to be touched in a rougher manner.

"You react quickly to stimulation. That is in your favor. You will do well here," she said.

"I won't do well here because I'm not staying," Piper snapped.

"Once the men take you, you will stay," Gemile smiled knowingly. "They are very experienced at pleasuring a woman, but only if you comply."

Shit! Were these chicks serious?

"Comply, my ass."

"You don't have a choice; you belong to the Death Valley Boys now."

"Sorry, but I belong to Jarod."

Their hands stilled on Piper's body.

"He has had you then. This is why you don't wish another man." Gemile whispered. "He is one of the most sensual sex slaves the women in Death Valley have ever encountered."

Most sensual sex slave? That son of a bitch! How many of these women did he service while he was here?

"He didn't leave Death Valley. He escaped," Lena spat.

"But he's back and perhaps we can have him again."

"Listen, ladies, this has been fun. Not. So, if you don't mind handing me my clothes, I'm outta here."

Piper made a quick move toward her clothing. She wasn't fast enough. Lena grabbed her arms yet again.

Shit!

"We will give you a glimpse at what happens to a woman who doesn't do what she is told," Gemile spat, and headed to a nearby door Piper hadn't noticed before.

She flung it open.

Piper gasped as she noticed a familiar red-haired woman standing bound and ball-gagged inside the closet. Her arms were up-stretched. Ropes coiled around her wrists and were looped around a horizontal pole near the ceiling. Her ankles were also secured with ropes to hooks in the floor.

It was the woman named Jasmine. The one she'd seen in the graveyard.

Piper swallowed at the red whip marks across the woman's generous breasts.

Her red hair was a tangled mess. Her face flushed with apparent anger. Pain filled Jasmine's round gray eyes, yet she stared defiantly at all of them.

"Worse will happen to you if you misbehave," Gemile cooed into Piper's ear.

"What…did she do?"

"She was caught masturbating after the Boys had taken her in the cemetery. Masturbating is not permitted. This is her punishment."

"Oh, come on! Is this really necessary?" Piper protested.

Gemile chuckled, "She'll think twice before she masturbates again."

"Maybe these Death Valley Boys don't please a woman as much as you brag if she has to resort to masturbating."

She didn't miss Jasmine's eyes twinkle with amusement at Piper's remark.

"If you are Jarod's woman, you won't be for long," Gemile growled. "The Death Valley Boys take any woman they want. No matter who she belongs to. They all share their women."

Piper swallowed at her suddenly dry throat as they dragged her into yet another room.

Two empty cages with black metal bars as thick as Piper's wrists stood side by side of each other and took up most of the cool candlelit room.

Each cage was at least seven-foot high and eight-foot-by-eight-foot wide with a cot complete with lumpy mattress and a pail on the floor.

One of the woman yanked open the creaking door to the nearest cage, and before Piper knew what was happening, they'd secured her chain to a hoop, snapped the padlock closed and pushed her roughly inside.

The door crashed shut behind her.

Her stomach plummeted at the squeaky grinding of the key in the lock. A quick glance around at the bars, and she knew there was no way she could escape this cage.

"The quicker you participate with the Death Valley Boys, the easier life will be for you," Gemile growled.

She grabbed the other woman by the arm and led her out of the room.

Piper should be freaking-out locked up in here with this irritating collar wrapped around her neck. She should be yelling and screaming, and demanding to be let out of here.

Strangely enough though, the only thing she could concentrate on at the moment was Jarod, and hoping his strength would come back quickly so they could get the hell out of here.

Piper shook her head in dismay.

What in the world was wrong with her anyway?

Her sisters were missing. She was on a mission to search for her brothers.

And all she could think about was some stranger. A hunky one-eyed man whose body and cock were riddled with scars. A sexy man who'd fucked her, quite beautifully she might add, against a tree under the moon glow on a godforsaken planet millions of miles from home.

She should have her head examined.

* * * * *

One day after Blackie had taken Piper away, Jarod was summoned to meet with the Council.

The instant he stepped inside the hide house containing the four selected members of the Council, he almost gagged. Pipe smoke hung heavy in the air, and it seeped like festering knots into his lungs and stung his eyes.

Five men including Blackie glared at him from their seated positions around a smoldering fire in the middle of the hide house. In a corner, he spotted a naked woman, sitting cross-legged. Tangles of red hair hid her face and her head was bowed, her hands in her lap.

It was High Queen Jasmine. He didn't miss the red whip welts crisscrossing her luscious breasts.

A flutter of compassion for the woman sifted through him. He wondered what she must have endured since he and Taylor had escaped. They'd wanted to take the gentle, compassionate High Queen with them, had wanted to protect her, but everything had happened so quickly back then and they hadn't been able to rescue her.

"Be seated, old friend," Blackie gestured to a tattered blanket on the dirt floor beside him.

Jarod took his place and accepted the smoking pipe.

He wished he didn't have to smoke it. But it would insult everyone if he refused and would only make a rotten situation worse.

Depending on the weeds they used, inhaling the smoke could produce hallucinations, all the way from telling the truth to immense sexual arousal. The last thing he wanted to do was slip up that Piper Hero didn't belong to him or to be sexually aroused enough to interfere with figuring out a way out of this mess.

But the other Boys were sucking on the pipe and they didn't appear to be disoriented.

When they handed it to him, he took a big drag and sucked in a huge puff of smoke into his lungs. Forcing himself to hold back a strangled cough, he exhaled slowly, acting as if he trusted these men. For good measure, he sucked in another round of smoke and passed the pipe to the next man.

A moment later, his body began to relax.

It was a good sign. It meant they were using the calming weed.

For a few minutes, all men remained silent as they took turns smoking the pipe.

When everyone had at least two turns, Blackie broke the silence.

"The warrior woman with you. She is a fighter. She killed our leader quickly and efficiently. Thankfully he did not suffer."

Jarod held back the urge to tell Blackie that Piper wasn't a killer. But he'd had time to think about things over the past day, and had come to the conclusion Piper was covering for her twin, Kinley. That could be the only explanation as to why Blackie thought Piper had killed the leader of the Death Valley Boys.

"The Boys had no idea who you were, Jarod," Blackie continued. "You were seen from behind and from far away. Once they saw the warrior woman who killed Laird they did not want to take any chances that she could escape again, and they acted quickly neutralizing both of you. We apologize for injuring you, Jarod. Eric didn't recognize you."

Jarod nodded.

The odd smirk on Eric's face led Jarod to believe Eric had known exactly whom he'd been targeting.

Jarod remembered the dark-haired man as being called Eric.

Eric was a troublemaker, a male with a hot temper. But he'd always managed to avoid the whip by framing someone else for his dirty deeds. He'd been one of the many males who'd broken from his group during the Slave Uprising and teamed with Laird, sexually taking women against their will.

Anger flared inside Jarod as he remembered their terrified and painful screams. The bruises and broken bones they'd suffered amongst other atrocities because Jarod hadn't been able to control Laird, Eric and the other males who'd mutinied.

Thankfully, the pipe was passed to him and he sucked in another round of smoke anxiously looking for the calming effect it would produce so he wouldn't break Eric's neck right then and there.

Fortunately, the curling smoke took the edge off his anger.

Jarod turned his attention to Blackie.

"Where is she?" he asked, although he knew exactly where they would put her.

"She is in the Shelter of the Cages. Unharmed as promised."

"I appreciate that you did not hurt my property."

"That is yet to be determined," another member growled.

"I for one am eager to fuck that warrior woman," Eric smiled smugly. "She is petite yet full of fire."

Jarod couldn't stop himself from clenching his fists as the anger grew another notch before being reined in by the calming effects of the inhaled smoke.

Three of these males, not including Blackie, were violent against women. There was no telling what they were capable of when it came to Piper.

Once again, the pipe was passed to him, and he drew in a deep puff of the scented smoke. It burned his lungs, yet thankfully continued to sooth his anger.

Blackie turned to the Council members. "A decision must be reached tonight regarding the woman."

"Never mind the female. A decision must be decided upon regarding Jarod," Eric snapped. "As far as I'm concerned he is not a member of us any longer. He and Taylor ran off. They deserted this membership. He has no rights. He must be killed or at the very least given back to Cath. I am sure she will be very grateful to have her pet sex slave back in her bedroom."

"That is out of the question for now," Blackie said coolly. "Jarod has challenged me for the woman."

"We don't do challenges anymore. Our traditions are to share," Eric snapped angrily.

"Death Valley traditions are to share but only if the male agrees," Jarod said coldly.

"That is how it was when you left. It has changed now," Blackie said softly.

A shiver ran up Jarod's spine.

"However," Blackie continued, "since you had no knowledge of this new tradition and since you were injured, I recommend we grant Jarod a reprieve. I recommend Jarod's life be spared, and that I be allowed to accept his challenge for the woman."

"Nonsense!" Eric snapped. "Jarod must die. There is a death bounty on his head."

The other men murmured with excitement, obviously not pleased with Blackie's suggestion.

"There is no leader therefore I am allowed to make these recommendations," Blackie said calmly.

Immediately, the men quieted down.

"If you let him back inside, he will try to change the traditions again. Just like the last time he was here," Eric snapped. "He was a weak leader during the Slave Uprising. He did not wish to harm the women. It was why he was recaptured by Cath. Why he suffered at her hand for a year. He only wishes to please women. He is still a sex slave."

Jarod stiffened at the insult. "I do not do what a woman says. I never will."

Eric turned to Blackie and the rest of the Council. "I am surprised he did not lead the woman here sooner. Now that she knows where we are, she will lead Cath here."

The blood in Jarod's entire body froze. He'd totally forgotten that angle.

"She was unconscious. She does not know where we are. She is not dangerous. I for one will accept Jarod into the fold. But if he decides to run again, he will be hunted down and killed. Is this acceptable?"

There was a round of murmurs accepting the decision.

"Eric? Is this acceptable to you?" Blackie asked.

Eric nodded and grinned savagely. "I look forward to hunting him down and killing him when he escapes again."

"What of the woman?" one of the men asked eagerly.

"Jarod must fight for her," Eric said smugly.

"He is not well enough to fight yet, Eric," Blackie protested.

"He will fight at sundown tomorrow," Eric said. "If not then he will die then. Since there is no leader this is my suggestion."

Silence overwhelmed the Council hut as the men thought over what Eric had stated.

Inwardly, Jarod cringed.

He wouldn't have a chance against Blackie, even if his shoulder wound had been fully healed.

While in captivity, they, as sex slaves, had been trained to fight for the amusement of the women. Blackie had won almost every fight against the other men. Thankfully, Jarod had never been made to fight his good friend but he had sparred with him during training, and he'd learned some of Blackie's weaknesses.

Jarod tried to keep his excitement from mounting. Perhaps he did have a slim chance at winning Piper.

"I will fight Jarod at sundown tomorrow. If it is agreeable to him," Blackie replied solemnly. Obviously, his old friend had just realized the same thing.

Jarod hesitated for effect then said, "It is agreeable."

Eric's smug smile widened. "Good. The fight will begin at sundown."

Chapter Nine

The ear-splitting sound of her cage door opening made Piper's eyes snap open.

She'd dozed off.

Nothing else to do in a cage but sleep, and dream of Jarod.

Blinking wildly into the semi-darkness, she noted a woman standing in the doorway.

"Good evening." The soft sultry voice was one she hadn't heard before. But Piper recognized the redhead right away.

Jasmine.

"What do you want?" Piper asked rather impolitely. Not that she felt like being polite after being totally naked, caged up like an animal for what seemed like eternity without someone to talk to except when they brought her something to eat.

"A decision has been made about your fate."

Oh, damn!

"Jarod and Blackie will fight each other for you."

Shit! Piper bolted up on the bed. Fury made her see red.

"Jarod's too ill to fight. God! What is it with you people? Is everyone so stupid around here that they can't figure it out?"

Frustration at this newest development made her feel like rushing the woman, escaping out the open door, grabbing Jarod and getting out of this nightmare. Unfortunately, the collar around her neck, and the chain secured to the cage prevented her from following her instincts.

"No need to worry about, Jarod. He is an excellent fighter. Besides he was given another quick healing injection, he will be fine."

"You saw him? How is he?"

"He has mended if the size of his arousal is any indication."

Piper blinked with surprise. "Arousal? What the hell do you mean by that?" If Jarod had been fucking these women, she'd never speak to him again.

"He became aroused while I sexually prepared him, just as I am here to do to you."

Sexually prepared him? What?

A riot of anger snapped along Piper's nerve. She resisted the urge to grab this woman's wild red curls and start pulling them out one-by-one.

"Exactly what did you do to sexually prepare him?"

Jasmine held up a glass jar filled with a clear liquid.

"What's that?"

"Preparation ointment to show off all your assets to the winner."

"Sorry, lady, but this chick is only going to Jarod." And maybe not even him if he'd been screwing around on her.

"Preparing you with the oil will also make it easier if the one you want doesn't win the fight," Jasmine said gently. "The oil contains a sensual herb that unleashes your sexual side and dulls your mind to rejecting a male. It will be easy for you to be impaled by a man not of your choosing."

"And what if I refuse to be…sexually prepared?"

"Then I will be punished."

Gee, no big surprise there. Those Death Valley Boys sure knew how to gnaw on someone's guilt.

She watched as Jasmine poured some oil from the glass jar onto her palms.

"Come, sit on the edge of the bed. We will begin."

Piper remained seated where she was, eying Jasmine warily. "What would your punishment be?"

"Usually when an assignment is not fulfilled, the woman is whipped. However, Blackie has made it quite clear that if my assignment is not carried out, I will be staked out in the middle of the village for twenty-four hours."

"That doesn't sound so bad."

"And the males will take turns fucking me all day and all night long. I may be addicted to sex, but I'm not that addicted. So, please, if you wouldn't mind allowing me to complete my assignment?"

Piper swore beneath her breath. Far be it for her to condemn this woman to more torment after she'd just spent time bound and gagged in a closet.

Exhaling a resigned sigh, she slid her feet over the edge of the bed and sat where Jasmine had indicated. "I'm only doing this so you won't be raped over and over again because of me."

"It wouldn't be rape." Jasmine knelt down at Piper's feet and lifted one of her feet into her lap beginning a slow sensual massage of the warm, slippery oil into the soles of her feet. "It would be punishment."

"Yeah, right, whatever." Was this woman screwed with her thinking or what? And she was supposed to be a queen? A woman with knowledge and here she was accepting this bull crap from these men.

"Jarod has told me that you come from somewhere else, from somewhere deep within the unexplored area of The Outer Limits, where your traditions are different than ours."

He did, did he? Well at least he'd kept his promise of not repeating what she'd told him under the influence of that passion scent he'd made her sniff.

"That's right."

"Then I will explain about the Death Valley Boys."

"No thanks, I know enough." Besides, she wouldn't be hanging around here for much longer. If there was a way out of here, she'd find it, sensual oil or no sensual oil. Jarod and she would be history the minute this collar was removed.

"The Death Valley Boys were sexual slaves."

"I know."

"Up until a little over three years ago, they only knew life as sexual objects. This is why their punishments are based on sex. Thankfully, though things are slowly changing since Blackie has become second in charge. We women are being allowed to educate the males. Most welcome their schooling. Some haven't accepted it."

An oddly pleasant sensation sizzled through the underneath areas on Piper's feet where Jasmine had applied the oil.

Wow, this tingling feeling sure did feel...really sexy.

"You said you did this to Jarod?"

"Yes."

"He let you?"

"He knows the rules of the Death Valley Boys."

Jasmine's fingers massaged oil into the tops of Piper's feet making her toes squirm at the ticklish sensations.

"Jarod is ticklish on his feet as well," Jasmine commented, as she poured more fluid onto her palms.

"Really?" She'd have to remember that. "Someone mentioned he was with the Death Valley Boys a couple of years back. Did you know him then?"

"Yes, he came here a few weeks before I arrived. When I met him, he was a very angry male. He appears to have changed."

"He has?"

Jasmine looked up at her with sparkling eyes. "When I met him, he used me often. Thrusting his demons into me, as if trying to be rid of them."

Piper blinked in shock. "Excuse me?"

"He and Blackie and Taylor were the first males who penetrated me."

"Like in ménage?"

She nodded and giggled. "Quite an amazing experience. One I wish could be repeated."

"I'll bet," Piper snapped.

"You need not worry. Jarod only has an eye for you."

"Really?"

Jasmine nodded.

"He mentioned you used to be a queen," Piper said suddenly, wanting to get to know more about this woman. "How come you're here? Why aren't you off leading your own people?" *And off fucking your own man instead of trying to fuck mine.*

"I helped a male named Ben Hero and my friend Queen Jacey escape prison."

Her brother had been in prison with a queen? Oh, boy, this story was getting good.

"Why were they in prison?"

"He's a male and he penetrated a queen. It is illegal."

"Well! Excuse me but I'm sure it must have been mutual consent!" Her brother did not go around fucking women who didn't want to be fucked.

Jasmine threw her an odd look and Piper realized she'd better settle down. Jasmine had no idea Ben was her brother.

"From what Jacey told me, she couldn't resist him. No matter, a queen who is penetrated by a male is ruined. She was trained to lead women and not allowed to be tarnished by a male in any way."

"You sure seemed to be enjoying all those men in the graveyard."

Jasmine's head snapped up.

Piper blushed. Maybe she should have kept her big mouth shut. But just the thought of this chick being with Jarod was really pissing her off.

"You observed?"

"We were hiding in some nearby bushes. We...um, couldn't help but notice the show."

Jasmine's fingers were sliding up the insides of Piper's knees heading toward a more intimate place.

"Lift your knees, place your feet on the edge of the bed and spread your legs, please."

Oh, heavens, this was getting a bit too much!

"Is this really necessary?" Piper asked, as she did what the woman instructed, trying very hard to ignore the coil of arousal sweeping through her lower abdomen as Jasmine's hands began to slide erotically up the insides of her thighs.

"You may be inspected thoroughly, I must not fail."

Oh, God! She didn't think she wanted to know exactly what this inspection might entail or who would be doing it.

"So, you said my brother and this queen were in prison because they...had sex. How come you aren't in prison? Why the Death Valley Boys?" And why the hell hadn't Ben come to this woman's rescue? Surely he would have returned the favor and saved her from her fate at the hands of the Death Valley Boys.

"The woman who took over Queen Jacey's position has many accomplices. She managed to get my prison sentence turned over, and sold me to the Breeders for quite a fair sum of money. The Breeders in turn trained me to...welcome sex. They then turned me over to the Death Valley Boys."

Piper stifled a whimper as Jasmine's oil-drenched fingers slid erotically against her pussy lips.

"I'm sure if you could arrange it so that Jarod and I could escape, we would take you with us. You wouldn't have to stay here and…service all those men."

Jasmine shook her head, her riot of red curls bouncing around. "I cannot leave here."

"Why not?"

"I have private reasons, but one reason I can share is this…"

Piper's lower abdomen clenched as Jasmine's fingers began a sensual rub against Piper's clitoris.

Oh, lady, that felt so good.

"I've been introduced into the world of sex. I cannot go without it for more than half a day before I need to have a male deep inside me."

"Jarod mentioned you women only get anal sex."

"Blackie knows my problem. He…helps me secretly."

Piper blew out a breath as the pleasant sensations played havoc with her morals. She shouldn't be allowing this woman to touch her this way. She should be reserving sex only for Jarod, but this sure felt good.

"What? You're saying you're addicted to sex?"

"What better place to get my daily fix than in a valley full of males?" Jasmine chuckled.

Piper groaned as Jasmine's lubricated finger slipped inside her channel. Her muscles clamped around the intrusion.

"The oil is doing the job," Jasmine commented, as she slid a second oil-drenched finger inside her vagina and massaged her G-spot.

"Did you do this to Jarod, too?" Piper gasped.

"Touch his penis?"

"Yes," Piper ground out when she couldn't stop gyrating her hips against the wonderful sensations Jasmine was creating.

"Yes. It is required. I have also prepared Blackie. You will do well with either one…or both, if the winner decrees it."

Piper swallowed. "What do you mean, both of them?"

"If Blackie wins, he has said he will share you with Jarod during the festivities. Jarod has told me he would prefer to keep you all to himself. Although I do not know how he can, considering the Death Valley Boys must share their women."

"Sorry lady, but I'm…a one-man kind of gal." Piper shivered her frustration as Jasmine's fingers slid out of her drenched vagina.

"Then you would most certainly prefer I don't bring you to orgasm?"

Oh, God!

"Did Jarod want you to?"

"No."

Shit! That son of bitch had more morals than she'd given him credit for.

"Then neither do I," she breathed, as her pussy trembled in disappointment.

Jasmine's oil-drenched hands sailed over her hairy muff, her fingers seductively massaging her abdomen and lower belly.

Suddenly the woman frowned. "You don't have a scar here. Blackie said you have a scar."

Oh, darn. She was screwed.

Suddenly her hands sensuously cupped Piper's mounds.

"You have nice-sized breasts," Jasmine continued without waiting for an explanation.

"Um…thank you."

"I always wished mine weren't so big," Jasmine said.

"I always wished mine were bigger."

The two women laughed.

To Piper's surprise, Jasmine began pinching and rolling her nipples between her fingers.

She couldn't stop her face from flaming nor could she stop her nipples from immediately hardening with arousal.

"You embarrass too easily. It may be difficult for you to be penetrated during the festivities by the winner."

Piper froze. "Exactly what do you mean by during?"

"The winner fucks the woman in front of everyone."

Oh, my God!

"I don't think so."

"Do not worry. The sensual oil will kick in by then. You won't care."

"I'll care afterwards."

"You will be fine. Trust me. They used the oils on me my very first time with Jarod and Taylor and Blackie and I wish—"

"I know already, you wish you could have them again."

Jasmine smiled softly.

Holy cow! If Jarod won, would he make love to her in front of all those people?

She didn't know if she should be screaming from shock or swooning with excitement. This planet was awesome. This free-wheeling way of sex stuff was all new to her and tough to digest. It was as if she was stuck in some erotic dream or something.

She almost wished she was.

At least then, she could relax and enjoy everything.

Jasmine reached for something out of the bag on the nearby shelf and returned her attention to Piper.

She watched Jasmine fiddle some more with her nipple until it felt rock-hard and burned, then she felt a tight squeeze and a pinch. A sweet pain zipped through her flesh and Piper couldn't help but gasp.

"These clamps will hurt slightly at first. You will get used to them."

A moment later her other nipple was clamped. Between the two clamps, Jasmine attached a few pretty gold chains that hung in different layers, the last layer hanging all the way down to her belly button.

"Your pale body contrasts well with the gold," Jasmine commented. "If you remove them, you and I both will be punished, so please keep them on."

"How's our newest female doing?"

Piper tensed as Blackie's voice reverberated throughout the room.

He stood just inside the door watching them intensely.

Jasmine visibly trembled. Whether out of fear or excitement, she wasn't sure. But by the way Jasmine's face lit up, she'd have to guess it was the latter.

"I am preparing her as you instructed. Feel free to inspect what I have done to her so far," Jasmine offered, as she stood away from Piper, who was still splayed out on the bed, her legs widespread with her cream of arousal seeping out of her, nipples swollen and red, and clamped with ornaments.

She swallowed hard at the look of lust brewing in Blackie's eyes as his gaze roved over her nude body.

Good grief. The way he looked at her was making her all hot and bothered.

What in the world would she do if he decided he wanted her now?

He was obviously already aroused and very naked. His giant cock stuck way up against his belly, his testicles hung so heavy and full, Piper shivered inwardly at the thought of being impaled by this man.

Strangely enough, it wasn't a shiver of revulsion, but of a shiver of curiosity as she remembered what Jasmine had said about Blackie sharing her with Jarod and Taylor.

The images of Jasmine being triple-penetrated blew into her mind. Taylor's cock tunneling up her ass, Blackie's massive shaft sinking into her tight pussy and Jarod getting orally done with her gorgeous full lips, drew in a sharp shocked breath from Piper, snapping her back to reality.

"I just came to show you what you'll be getting when I win the fight," Blackie drawled.

Piper's fists clenched in anger as she quickly sat up on the bed, drew her legs closed against herself hiding her breasts and her nonexistent scar from his view.

"Don't be so cocksure of yourself, Mr. Blackie. Jarod will win."

"We will see. And I will enjoy running my tongue over that scar on your abdomen."

"Dream on, mister."

Jasmine threw Piper a strange look, and she hoped Jasmine would keep her mouth shut about not seeing a scar.

Blackie chuckled, and Piper couldn't help but lose some of her tension at the soft sound of his laugh. Instincts were whispering to her that this guy wasn't as tough as he was letting on.

"I will not have any time to dream when you are cradled in my arms and my cock and Jarod's shaft are penetrating you. Simply ask Jasmine. She must have told you that Jarod and I and Taylor were her first males?"

A stab of jealousy zipped along her nerves yet she kept quiet.

Blackie turned to Jasmine. "I need you to apply some more oil to me. You can finish her off later."

Jasmine nodded. Piper didn't miss the sparkle of arousal sweep over the ex-High Queen's face.

"Over there. In the next cage," Blackie instructed.

Piper's heart picked up a rapid speed as she watched Jasmine pad barefoot from her cage giving her a close-up view of a large gold anal ring glistening between her plump ass cheeks.

Jarod had been right. They had outfitted Jasmine with an anal ring.

Jasmine entered the cage next door with Blackie right behind her.

He lay down on the narrow cot, his long powerful legs widespread and outstretched. His arms bulged beautifully as he clamped them beneath his neck and watched Jasmine begin her sensual massage.

Piper didn't know if it was appropriate or bad manners to watch, but what they were doing here certainly wasn't the best etiquette so she decided this was the perfect opportunity to see what Jasmine had done to Jarod.

She did exactly the same thing as she'd done to her.

Starting at the toes, massaging his feet, ankles, muscular legs, thighs.

When Jasmine poured the sensual oil upon Blackie's swollen testicles, he closed his eyes and sighed heavily. "Jasmine, you are the best."

She smiled softly at him.

Her big breasts jiggled sensuously as her fingers kneaded his oil-shined scrotum.

A low groan rumbled somewhere deep in his chest.

Piper watched as his cock grew even larger beneath Jasmine's fingers. Veins pulsed. His flesh shaded a deep purple.

Have mercy but he was just as big as Jarod.

Arousal shifted through Piper's veins at the erotic sight. She found herself envisioning Jarod lying on the bed with Jasmine's fingers toying with his cock.

Had Jarod's cock pulsed beneath the woman's hands? Had his balls swelled as big and hard-looking as Blackie's?

Piper swallowed back a strangled sob, and tried to stem the tide of arousal shifting through her hot body as she watched Jasmine's head lower. She opened her mouth.

Clenching her teeth with frustration, Piper watched as Blackie's swollen mushroom-shaped head slipped between Jasmine's eager, full lips.

Had Jasmine done this to Jarod?

Oh, man, she was really being stupid about all this. She'd had sexual intercourse with Jarod once, and she was already thinking of him as her man.

She needed to get a reality check.

The erotic sounds of Jasmine sucking on Blackie's cock brought back memories of that one night she'd done the same thing to Jarod.

God, they'd been so hot for each other. She'd thought for sure he would have taken her right then and there up against the wall of the tree house.

The anger in his eyes had surprised her but now she finally understood.

Jarod had been a sex slave. Raised from childhood to be one.

From what the women who'd given her a bath had said, men had been kept in cages similar to this one almost their entire life.

Women had told Jarod what to do. Women had demanded sex from him. And a woman named Cath had tortured him as well.

God! How he must hate women for making his life a living hell.

Yet, he didn't hate her. He'd come looking for her when she'd struck out from the tree house on her own. He'd saved her by throwing her behind the bushes seconds before those Death Valley Boys had shown up in the graveyard. He'd dragged her out of that cemetery telling her it was too dangerous to go through it.

He wouldn't do that if he didn't care about her.

At the erotic sounds of Blackie's groans, Piper's fingers slid between her drenched thighs and began a slow rub on her puffy clitoris.

She was ultra-sensitive from Jasmine's sensual touches and the oil she'd covered her body with, and it didn't take her long before her breath grew heavy and exquisite sensations began unraveling throughout her body.

From the cage next door, she watched Jasmine release his enlarged cock and climb onto the bed. Straddling her legs on each side of Blackie's torso, she lowered herself slowly.

Piper found herself crying out at the sight of his swollen cock disappearing between Jasmine's large pussy folds. Jasmine sucked in a harsh breath and then let herself go, impaling her drenched cunt onto Blackie.

Sensual sensations whipped around Piper as she watched Jasmine's full hips gyrate.

Piper's slippery fingers continued rubbing her soaked clit. Her other hand smoothed over her hard breasts and grabbed onto one of her nipple clamps.

She bit her bottom lip at the sweet pain blossoming there as she twisted the metal.

From the other cage, Blackie's erotic groans rippled through the air, followed by Jasmine's soft cries of arousal. The sucking sound of her pussy enveloping his rigid flesh as she pumped her hips into him zapped through the air.

Piper in turn pictured herself pumping her hips into Jarod, her hot cunt encircling Jarod's hot, thick cock. His swollen balls slapping hard against her quivering flesh as he thrust into her, impaling her against that tree.

Piper spread her legs wider, her fingers moving faster over her slippery swollen clitoris.

The sweet sensations broke free from her in a gasp.

She rode her hand hard, pretending it was Jarod. Pretending that he was fucking her so hard, he was making her scream.

Erotic pleasure cascaded over her in silver streaks making Piper grimace as the fantastic orgasm consumed her.

Her hips gyrated.

Her breasts bounced back and forth.

Her mouth fell open allowing her aroused gasps to escape her feverish body.

Oh, God! Jarod, where are you? her mind cried out as the sensations swirled all around her.

They felt so good. Oh, yes, so good.

But she wished Jarod was here fucking her. Wished he'd win the fight and would take her in front of all those people.

"Jarod!" she cried out into her cage as she came hard. "Oh, God! Jarod!"

Her body shook with the pleasure.

Her mind cried at the loss of Jarod not being here to share this fantastic orgasm with her.

When the climax drifted away, she was surprised to hear silence permeate the room.

Wearily she turned her head.

Both Jasmine and Blackie, who'd completed their fucking session, their bodies drenched in perspiration were staring at her with wondrous looks on their faces.

Oh, God!

She'd just masturbated in front of these two.

As if Blackie was thinking the same thing, he grinned lustily at her. "Good practice for later."

She wanted to tell him to go fuck himself, but didn't think that would go over too well.

At that moment, she wished she had a blanket to cover herself.

She didn't. So she merely gave him the middle finger when he returned his attention to watching Jasmine's breasts sway as she remained impaled on his rod and picked up where she'd left off and began massaging the oil into Blackie's belly.

* * * * *

Jarod's heart pounded violently when he saw them bring Piper to the side of the ring where the fight was to take place.

They'd taken her clothing and greased her sensual curves making her look like a goddess.

He reined in his anger as he noted the men's lusty gazes riveted to her nakedness. She wore golden nipple clamps with chains. Her cunt was shaven and gold glinted down there. Obviously, she'd been fitted with labial clamps as well.

Her hair was swept off her neck and was piled prettily on top of her head.

She looked scared.

And she looked absolutely ravenous.

He had to win this fight.

Needed to make sure the other men didn't touch her.

He needed her for himself.

A cheer went up through the crowd and Jarod forced himself to look away from Piper, and discovered Blackie entering the fight ring.

The fight was about to begin.

Blackie wore nothing but the traditional fighting breechclout, an ultra-thick material that helped protect a Death Valley male's cock and balls during a fight. The cloth barely hid his swollen sex. Obviously, he was aroused and thinking that in Jarod's weakened condition, he'd have a good chance to win the fight.

Blackie's body glistened with oil as well, illuminating the bunched muscles in his legs as he walked confidently into the middle of the ring where Jarod stood.

Jarod nodded a greeting.

"You still have a chance to change your mind, Jarod. You aren't in your best form for a fight," Blackie said quietly, so that only the two of them heard. "You can concede to me and I'll be gentle with her, train her for the other men."

"She's mine," Jarod stated firmly.

Blackie nodded.

Jarod kept his gaze on Blackie, and waited for the signal.

When it came, Jarod was ready.

Ducking a quick swing from Blackie, he kneed him in the solar plexus. His opponent doubled over, and Jarod clubbed him with clasped hands on the back of his neck.

Blackie fell to his knees with a grunt, but before Jarod could escape, Blackie grabbed him by the hips, pushing Jarod down onto his back. Blackie came barreling down on top of him, knocking the wind out of his lungs.

The men cheered.

Blackie grinned, "Easy win."

Fury raged inside Jarod and he hissed coldly, "For me."

With a cry of anger, Jarod bumped his forehead against Blackie's face with all his might.

Pain lunged through Jarod's head and stars exploded behind his eye. A loud crack rippled through the air as Blackie's nose broke.

Jarod winced at his old friend's anguished cry, but there was no time for compassion.

The instant he felt a shift in Blackie's weight, Jarod pushed him aside and scrambled to his feet.

The crowd booed.

Despite the pain Blackie must be feeling, he rolled easily to his feet.

The crowd roared.

Swaying, Blackie grinned at him, and wiped away a string of blood that dribbled from his nose.

"The woman must be a good fuck," Blackie said softly, so only the two men could hear.

"She's worth fighting for."

"I agree."

"You'll not get her," Jarod warned.

"We'll see."

They circled around each other until the crowd grew restless.

Jarod could feel the weakness seeping slowly into his body as the evening heat scrambled into his pores. Sweat popped out on his back and dribbled into his eye. He blinked it away quickly.

He wouldn't be able to fight too much longer. It was time to put an end to this nonsense, and he knew exactly how to do it.

He accepted a few quick jabs from Blackie.

Then went in for the kill.

Blackie had a bad shoulder. If he twisted it just right...

Strangely enough, it was easy grabbing him by his bad arm, almost as if he'd been expecting Jarod to do it.

He didn't have time to think about his good fortune, though, and with a mighty twist and a quick yank the deed was done.

Jarod winced as Blackie howled with pain.

With Blackie's arm now hanging uselessly at his side, Jarod gave him the final blow by tripping him.

He fell to the ground and dust sprung up around them. In a flash, Jarod knelt onto Blackie's chest, pushing hard and preventing him from getting up.

"Do you yield?" he yelled at his fallen opponent.

"I yield!" Blackie shouted, and grimaced with pain.

To Jarod's surprise, the crowd cheered.

He smiled.

He had won the fight.

Gazing over at Piper, Jarod's smile froze when he saw Eric holding her in his grasp, a knife to her neck.

The crowd stilled.

"You have won the fight, Jarod. And now you must claim her in front of all to see. It is tradition."

Jarod nodded in agreement. He could only hope that Piper understood the way of the Death Valley Boys and wouldn't hate him when all was over.

* * * * *

Keep calm. That's all you have to do. Just keep your cool, Piper told herself as she felt the cool blade of the knife pressed against her neck.

When Jasmine had finished with Blackie and returned to finish preparing Piper for the winner, she'd explained everything that Piper should expect after the fight.

Despite the fact she knew what was expected of her, Piper had still been shocked to be paraded naked in front of so many men.

Although it was obviously quite common here, this stuff just didn't happen back on Earth. She had to repeat it to herself over and over that she was millions of miles from home, and these men were used to seeing women naked. They were runaway sex slaves, for heaven's sake.

Besides, no one would have to know about this sexual escapade when she went back home. Her reputation would still be intact. In the meantime, she would just treat this as some erotic adventure.

When Jarod neared her, she felt the knife slide away from her throat and the man who held her let her go.

"Take her, now, Jarod." The man grinned.

She couldn't stop her breath from quickening as Jarod's appreciative gaze watched her intently. His nearness aroused her, and now as she stood in front of all these men and women the reaction to him was just as powerful, perhaps even more than the first time she'd awoken with Jarod's head between her legs.

Jasmine had said the oil she'd massaged into Piper's skin would make her accept whoever won, but she was truly glad that it was Jarod.

"Let's pretend it is the two of us. They will join us soon enough."

Yes, Jasmine had said it was only mandatory for them to watch the penetration. Then the males would take their women, and Jarod and Piper would just be part of the crowd having sex.

When he held out his hand, she took it immediately.

His fingers felt ultra hot as they slid against her palm.

He smiled and tugged her into the ring.

"We have no choice, do you understand?" Jarod whispered.

Piper nodded.

"I apologize for this."

"Don't apologize. I came all these millions of miles for an adventure, and I haven't regretted a minute of it. I'm just glad you're all right and that you won me," Piper admitted truthfully.

"Are you ready?"

She nodded, feeling nervous but exquisitely excited as well.

Jasmine had told her she was extremely lucky because new traditions said Death Valley Boys were supposed to share their women. It was a sign to show the males that they were not attached to women. But Jasmine had warned, it would only be a matter of time before the males challenged Jarod and then he would have to share her.

That's why she'd been so scared when that man had pulled the knife on her. She'd thought Jarod was being challenged.

Cheers flew into the air from the spectators and her eyes widened as Jarod suddenly dropped the breechclout from around his hips.

God! But the man was built. And even with all these people watching them, he was fully erect.

Did publicly displaying himself turn him on? Or was he aroused because of her?

She didn't have time to ponder the questions because he smiled and Piper's heart picked up speed.

"You know what to do."

She nodded.

At that moment she felt the various clamps Jasmine had outfitted her with tingle to life.

Her nipple clamps vibrated wonderfully.

Her labia clamps pulsed.

The clit clamps forced incredible pleasure to swoop through her.

She knew Jasmine held the controls. Knew she would stimulate her so Jarod could concentrate on the impalement, giving the onlookers a show they won't soon forget.

Piper swallowed nervously and did what Jasmine had instructed her to do.

Getting down on all fours, she closed her eyes and waited.

She tensed as something hot slid against the tight opening of her asshole.

"Stay calm. Concentrate on what I'm doing to you," he whispered.

She nodded.

Tuning out the leering men's faces and the excited wide-eyed looks of the women who stood beside the men, Piper concentrated on the sensuous vibrations of the clamps and the erotic way Jarod's hands were smoothing over the curves of her buttocks.

Jasmine had told her not to worry about being anally injured by Jarod's huge rod. All males were instructed to liberally lubricate their cocks with a special ointment that allowed a woman's anal muscles to stretch to unbelievable proportions without injury. So she wasn't afraid of being injured without being prepared with a butt plug.

What frightened her were the erotic sensations screaming through her at the thought of all these people watching her. She'd heard about people having sex in places where they might be caught, but she'd never tried it with the few men she'd slept with.

Perhaps the ointment Jasmine had smoothed over her body had increased the desires that had lain dormant inside her all these years.

She gasped as she felt pressure as Jarod's thick mushroom-shaped cock started to invade her virgin ass.

The pressure increased.

She gasped at the wild sensations as her sphincter muscle gave way, and his lubricated cock slipped inside her.

Jarod's hands were erotically massaging the curves of her ass cheeks now. The intimate gesture made her believe it was his way of keeping her calm, keeping what was happening intimate.

Pleasure-pain slid along the tunnel of her ass as he continued his slow impalement.

Her clit clamp made her squirm.

She fought the insane urge to squeeze her legs together and press herself to an orgasm on her own.

She kept her eyes clenched tightly as the incredible pleasure-pain zipped through her.

The vibrating clamps increased in their intensity.

Her clit burned.

Ached.

Trembled.

Warm pleasure cream seeped from her vagina. A vagina that quivered, and needed to be filled.

Now she understood what Jarod had said about why men were only allowed to fuck a woman in the ass unless it was for breeding purposes.

An anal impalement was so different than a vaginal penetration.

It left her feeling needy.

Feeling desperate to have her cunt filled by him.

Jarod's lubricated cock slid deeper up her ass.

Incredible pressure seared through her, accompanied by the sweet pleasure-pain that had her gasping. Had her squirming. Trembling.

He filled her ass beautifully, and she was being consumed with erotic sensations she'd never felt before. She could feel the impending climax awakening. Gathering speed. Hurrying toward her.

Her heart thumped wildly as Jarod groaned. It was a wild sound. A sound that made her instinctively whimper in answer.

His big cock slid deeper, parting her virgin ass muscles, stretching her, coaxing more whimpers from her mouth.

Blood roared in her ears drowning out the cheers of the men as Jarod's cock sunk deeper.

His warm palms continued to stroke her ass tenderly.

Lovingly.

His voice sounded soothing as he whispered calming words.

It felt so good to have her tender ass swallowing his long, thick cock. It was so unbelievably different than anything she'd ever experienced, yet at the same time her pussy wept and begged for him, too.

He was withdrawing now, her velvet anal walls protesting as he slid out.

She bit her lip, her ass clenching wonderfully against him as he thrust into her ass again in one solid blissful thrust.

Oh, God!

The vibrating clamps powered against her flesh, bringing a flood of sensual sensations.

Jarod slammed into her ass again.

And again.

The climax neared.

Her cunt dripped with warm pleasure juices that ran down the insides of her thighs.

The force of his thrusts increased.

Pushing her toward the dangerous edge of erotic bliss.

The wonderful edge where she knew she'd find relief.

She dug her fingers into the ground. Wished her hands were clenched around Jarod's neck as he thrust into her.

The edge arrived and she washed over it.

Indescribable pleasure racked her.

Powerful explosions slammed into her. Twisting her. Breaking her.

She felt feverish. Her body inundated with exquisite pleasure-pain.

She cried out her arousal.

Bright stars exploded behind her eyes.

Through the erotic haze of bliss, she heard Jarod answer in his guttural groans as he fucked her ass.

His cock burned into her very depths.

She jerked wildly. Every part of her crying out her pleasure.

He drove harder. Wilder.

His ravaging thrusts made her asshole clench tighter around his intrusion. Her pussy spasmed.

Oh, God! It was sweetly mind-blowing.

She screamed and shuddered as he continued to pump into her.

Incredible waves washed over her, lifting her higher and higher, forcing the agonizing cries of her arousal from somewhere deep in her very soul.

The waves engulfed her.

Tortured her.

Made love to her.

Just when she thought one was finished another sensual wave racked her.

Finally, his cock scalded her, pouring his semen deep into her ass.

By the time he was finished with her, she was an exhausted trembling ball of whimpers.

She barely felt him lift her into his warm arms.

Her eyes fluttered open, and she saw men and women all around them. Women on all fours like she'd been, while the men fucked them doggie-style.

It was an awesome sight.

Amazing.

She wished she could watch, but she was so tired.

"You okay?" Jarod purred into her ear.

She moaned and nodded, snuggling into his wet chest, smelling the wonderful scent of his male perspiration.

"We have been given Blackie's lodge for tonight. Now we can plan how to escape," he whispered.

She nodded wearily.

She didn't even want to think of an escape right now. Something dark hovered at the back of her mind. It was nudging her toward asking Jarod to stay here in Death Valley so she could experience this erotic bliss every day.

It would be a dream come true.

Snuggling her head against the curve of his damp muscular shoulder, she swiftly fell asleep.

* * * * *

Watching Piper sleep, her naked body nestled upon the lush bear skin where he'd placed her after taking her from the fight ring, made an unwanted warmth curl through Jarod's heart.

She was a most amazing woman.

No other woman would have participated so boldly in a public fucking ceremony especially on her first time.

She'd been so giving. So perfect.

He couldn't help but wonder how his heart had melted so quickly against her; and with the warmth flowing in his heart, he was beginning to lose his perspective of revenge against women in general.

He couldn't afford to wallow in these fascinating feelings toward her. He needed to rebuild the ice wall around his heart, and find a way to make Cath and the women of Merik free all males.

And he couldn't do it by indulging himself in the warmth of this woman.

And he couldn't do it by lounging around in Death Valley.

* * * * *

Piper didn't comprehend the soft sound of footsteps nearby. Nor did she fully awake.

Not until the strong, hot hand clamped tightly over her mouth.

She bolted when she spotted the dark eyes of Blackie staring down at her.

Dark menacing eyes that frightened her.

Oh, God!

Was he here to challenge Jarod again? Or was he here to kidnap her, and take her to the other men like Jasmine had warned could happen?

Surely, Jarod wouldn't allow it.

It didn't take but a split second for her to realize Jarod wasn't even in the hide house.

Before she could even think to struggle, Blackie said something that made the blood freeze in her veins.

"Keep quiet, or Jarod is a dead man."

* * * * *

The instant he left the shelter, Jarod knew someone followed him. His first instincts had been to dive back into the lodge and protect Piper. But he had the feeling whoever was out there wanted him out of the way first.

He wasn't wrong.

When he entered the nearby bushes, three males emerged and quickly surrounded him.

"Going somewhere?" Eric cooed softly.

Jarod didn't miss the long, deadly knives all three men brandished in their hands.

"Does it break the rules of the Death Valley Boys to relieve oneself?" Jarod asked tightly, preparing himself for a fight.

"You should have emptied yourself in the female. That's what she's here for," Eric grinned evilly.

Jarod stemmed his rising anger at the comment. Eric was merely baiting him, trying to anger him so Jarod would strike out blindly.

He braced himself as one of the men circled behind him out of his field of vision. Ever since he'd lost one eye, he'd made it a habit to rely on his hearing skills and now his ears kicked in full swing.

The footsteps didn't come any closer. He wondered if perhaps the male would await a signal from Eric.

"Don't worry, Jarod. The three of us will fill her up for you. From the way she enjoyed today's coupling with you, we have decided not to bother to challenge you for the female. It will be easier to kill you now."

"Go ahead and try."

"You seem eager to die, Jarod. Was she not a good fuck?" Eric smirked.

The anger brewing inside Jarod notched up a degree. Eric and the other man in front of him circled closer, their deadly knives flashed in the moonlight.

"You'll never find out," Jarod said tightly. He would fight until the death in order to protect Piper.

"By the sounds of her moans while you plunged into her, she seems a sensual creature." Eric lunged at Jarod with the knife.

Jarod easily sidestepped the attack.

The other man behind him hung back, confirming Jarod's suspicions. He needn't worry about the other two just yet. Eric wanted a try at him first.

"Perhaps purchasing women from the Breeders is not in the best interest of the Death Valley Boys? Perhaps we should raid the surrounding hubs and get ourselves some spirited women like this Piper woman? Or like the women we fucked during the Slave Uprising? They fought hard but we were stronger."

"Strength proves nothing," Jarod said.

"It proves we can dominate the female and not the other way around," Eric retorted.

"It proves you have no brains, Eric."

In the moonlight, he could see Eric's face flush with anger.

"You are the one without brains, Jarod. Or you wouldn't have lost your leadership during the Slave Uprising. Or your eye afterwards…"

Jarod refused to bite the bait.

"What else did those women do to you, Jarod? Did you enjoy those heavy weights they hung from your balls? Is that why they're so big now? You must be into torture that could account for all those scars you so proudly wear on your body."

"Are you jealous, Eric? Seems to me, you were the one eager to kiss the women's feet back at the women's villages in order to avoid a whipping. Is that why you don't have any scars?"

The man accompanying Eric shifted his position and the one behind Jarod took a step away from Jarod. Where they pondering what he'd just said?

"Enough of this idle talk. Prepare to die," Eric snapped.

He nodded to his males, and all three started to close in around Jarod.

Jarod tensed, readying himself for combat, his mind quickly formulating and casting aside plans of defense on how he could make it out of this confrontation alive.

Three-to-one were not good odds.

Especially when he was defenseless and they brandished knives.

Without warning one of the men slumped to the ground, an axe buried deep in his back.

Eric and the other male stopped, looking at their fallen comrade with bewilderment.

There wasn't any time to ponder who was helping him so Jarod quickly pounced into action.

Ripping the axe from the fallen male's back, he easily slashed the nearest male's throat.

A horrible gurgling sound emerged from the male and he fell to the ground, blood gushing from his throat wound.

Eric, ever the coward, turned to run but stopped short when an arrow zipped through his upper back.

His eyes grew wide and a soundless scream erupted from his throat.

Without a word, he fell to his knees and then collapsed.

Jarod whirled around ready to fight the unknown assailant, and was stunned to find Blackie standing there, a bow in his hand; an ugly blue bruise decorated the base of his nose.

Behind him stood a beautiful white horse.

Piper sat astride the creature, her dark hair tangled and mussed from sleep, sliding like a waterfall over a thin sheet that engulfed her upper body, her naked legs clenching the sides of the stallion.

"Are you all right?" she whispered, her sweet lips trembled as if she was about to cry.

He could literally feel her concerned gaze raking over every part of him to make sure he hadn't been injured. To his surprise, it made him feel good to have a female worried about his safety.

"They did not harm me," he reassured her. "Are you fine?"

She nodded. "I was just afraid of what might have happened to you. Jasmine said anyone could challenge you for me."

"No one will challenge Jarod as long as you both leave at once," Blackie said, and thrust the reins of the stallion into Jarod's hand.

"Thank you, Blackie, for saving my life."

Blackie cracked a grin. "It was my pleasure."

"I also apologize for your breaking your nose."

He shrugged. "I've had worse. It will heal."

"You are welcome to come with us. Taylor and I have a tree house. It is well-hidden. You could stay there with us. It is safe enough. Away from all this madness and from what you have to do for Cath."

"I cannot."

"Why not? It is obvious you do not like the circumstances here. That is why you allowed me to win the fight so easily. Come with us, now. Be safe."

Blackie's grin widened, and for a moment, Jarod caught a glimpse of his good-natured old friend.

"Take the woman, and leave before someone realizes you are missing."

The firmness in his voice made him realize Blackie wouldn't be budged. Quickly, he hoisted himself onto the broad back in front of Piper. Immediately, her arms curled around his waist and held him tight.

Just feeling the lush curves of her breasts pressing against his back made an emotion so strong uncoil inside him, he felt certain his heart would have died if anything bad had happened to her here.

"I thank you for giving us our freedom," Jarod replied.

"Consider it for old times' sake."

"Will you be safe here? How will you explain the missing horse?"

"I will tell them you stole it. Is it not the truth?"

Jarod chuckled, and Blackie smiled softly.

"Safe journey, old friend. And ride like the wind, for they will surely follow."

He nodded, and with a brief wave, he kicked the white stallion into action.

Chapter Ten

They rode furiously all night, nibbling on the food Blackie had provided for them. The next day, Jarod kept the horse at a quick trot allowing frequent short breaks as they followed the river systems.

When he felt sure no one followed, he steered the stallion back onto land, and headed directly north toward the hills and the valley beyond.

Behind him, Piper remained silent, her arms wrapped snugly around his waist, her breasts pressed intimately against his back and her chin tucked snugly on his shoulder as they shared frequent and passionate kisses.

Finally, on the eve of the second day, she reached down and boldly fondled his hardened sack with her fingers.

"You better be careful with that precious cargo, Piper," Jarod chuckled at her.

"Is it true what Eric said? Did the women really hang weights from your balls?" she asked, her supple lips teasing the base of his neck.

"Among other places," Jarod said softly, trying hard not to give in to the molten desires whirling through him.

He wanted to ride a little while longer. Just to be on the safe side. But the way Piper's soft hands splayed across his bare chest and tweaked his nipples, his resolve was quickly fading.

"And were you aroused with those weights hanging off your balls?"

"Sometimes."

"And the other times?"

"It hurt."

She kneaded his hard balls and Jarod's breath quickened.

"Does it hurt when I touch you now?"

"No, it pleases me."

"And it pleases you when I do this?" She nibbled intimately on his earlobe, and continued to knead his balls at the same time.

Heated arousal zipped through his cock.

"Wherever you touch me pleases me."

"Good answer," Piper said, and brushed her lips against his strong jaw. "Where are we heading anyway?"

"I'm taking you to the valley where your brothers are living."

"You finally trust me?"

"I wouldn't have fought for you and fucked you in front of all those men if I didn't trust you, Piper."

"Mmm. Another good answer."

Her hands left his balls, and wrapped snugly around the base of his swollen cock.

"Piper…" he warned.

"What?" she whispered, her voice sounding hot and sexy.

"I'll show you what!" he roared.

The need that had been building in him since they'd left Death Valley finally exploded. Without another word, he brought the stallion to a standstill and hopped off.

* * * * *

Piper giggled as he curled his arm around her waist and roughly dragged her from the horse.

"Oh, I like it when you're rough."

"I thought you said I was a knight in shining armor and they are supposed to be gentle."

She grinned teasingly, loving the way his hot gaze sliced deep into her very soul, heating her core and making her cunt cream warmly.

"Doesn't mean you have to be gentle with me."

"I'm going to fuck you now. Sweet and gentle. Hard and rough. Any way you like it. Any objections?"

"Is that your way of telling me you like me?"

A puzzled wrinkle burrowed in his forehead. "Is that what this interesting feeling is called?"

"Interesting? I think I have better words—"

His head dipped, and he crushed his warm mouth to her lips cutting her off.

He tasted hot, dark and dangerously wonderful.

His tongue speared into her mouth, making her stagger from the scorching onslaught of emotions cascading through her. She grabbed his big shoulders, steadying herself and cried out as she felt the hard bulge of his loincloth-covered erection press intimately against her pussy. Grinding her hips, she pressed her clit against his heavy erection, and groaned into his mouth as pleasure sparkled around her.

To her frustration, he broke the kiss, and his hot breath fanned her face.

"I am still learning the language of Merik, my words are limited. So I thought it best to show you how I feel, instead of using words."

"They say the language of love knows no boundaries. Lovemaking makes up for the lack of words," she said, as she continued to grind her pussy into his hard bulge.

"I think I will enjoy this lovemaking," he purred, as his fingers slid against her palm. Leading her by the hand, he took her to a nearby hollow filled with sweet-smelling wildflowers.

The instant they reached it, he slipped the sheet from her shoulder and let it drift to the ground.

A hot flush swept through her as his gorgeous blue eye skimmed over her nakedness.

"How do you wish me to fuck you this time?" he asked softly, his eye darkening with lust.

"I want it rough and hard," she whispered, watching the way his tongue swiped hungrily at his bottom lip as he continued that luscious hot stare.

"As rough as you want it or as rough as I want it?"

She swallowed at his question. "As you want it."

He was breathing hard now. His gorgeous erection pressing so hard against his loincloth she felt sure his cock would rip right through the thin material.

"Lie down in the grass. I will be back in a moment," he said, and started toward the horse. Toward the sack of food Blackie had packed for them.

He was picking an odd time to go and get something to eat.

"I'm not hungry," she called out after him.

"Lie down," he growled. "Scrunch your sheet into a ball and place it beneath your hips. Knees up. Spread your legs wide for me. Very wide."

Oh, my gosh! What did he have in mind for her?

She blew out a tense breath, and did as he instructed. Lying down on the sweet-smelling grass, she scrunched up the sheet and placed it comfortably beneath her. The rolled-up sheet lifted her hips perfectly, giving him full access to her.

Bracing her knees upward, she spread her legs and planted her feet into the cool grass. Then she waited.

The sky above her shimmered a pretty pale blue as the sun set behind the lush jungle of trees. A mild late evening breeze caressed her sopping pussy, and spilled against her sore ass making her remember the sensual way he'd impaled her ass the other day in front of the Death Valley Boys. Made her remember how the men and women had hungrily watched the penetration before she'd closed her own eyes, and allowed herself to drift into the wondrous thing Jarod had been doing to her ass.

Eagerness gripped her. She wanted to be vaginally penetrated by him. And now that she'd been anally penetrated, she wanted that, too.

Which would he do to her first?

When she heard him coming, she couldn't stop herself from trembling at the intense need coursing through her every fiber. Couldn't stop herself from touching her breasts, from tugging and pinching her nipples until they burned hard and red for him.

And she couldn't stop those fever sex dreams from zipping into her mind.

She inhaled at the intensity of them, at the shadowy silhouette of Jarod standing between her widespread legs, his head lowering between them. Couldn't forget how hard her heart had pounded against her chest as she'd sobbed and begged him to penetrate her.

It was all coming back to her now.

The feverish, killer heat sliding over her skin. The hot perspiration drenching her.

At the time, she hadn't known she'd been caught in the fever sex dreams. Had only wanted relief from the sexual agony thrusting through her entire body. Hadn't cared who would fuck her.

She remembered seeing Taylor coming into the tree house room several times while she'd screamed and orgasmed, remembered how he'd thrown envious looks at his friend as Jarod had sucked wildly at her clit. Most of all she remembered the powerful relief Jarod's hot tongue had allowed her as he'd furiously sucked the pleasure juices from her body, giving her endless orgasms.

Jarod had been so protective of her, never leaving her side, never allowing his friend to touch her no matter how hard she'd begged both of them to fuck her.

How she would ever face Taylor again without flushing with embarrassment, she had no idea. Maybe it would have been better if she hadn't remembered.

A shadow moved in front of her and her fingers stilled on her breasts.

Jarod stood there.

Feasting his eye between her widespread legs making her burn at the intense way he stared. It was almost more than she could bear.

Pleasure juices slid down her channel, readying her for penetration. Delicious sensations hummed through her body.

Suddenly his loincloth fell away and she saw his testicles, heavy and swollen with his seed. His huge cock flushed red and angry, it vibrated as he watched her, the thick web of veins pulsing, his swollen cock head bulging from his sheath. A pearly drop of pre-come appeared at the tiny slit.

"You're remembering the fever sex dreams," he whispered. "I can see it in your eyes. In the way you look at me. Just as you looked at me all those times you wanted me to fuck you during your fever sex dreams. And I can see it in the way your cream drips from your pussy."

He stepped closer.

She held her breath and waited anxiously for his next move, and caught the sunlight twinkle off something gold in his hand.

Gold chains dangled from his hand.

Oh, God! He held the vibrating clamps Jasmine had placed on her nipples, and labia and clit along with the tiny control box.

"Where'd you get those?"

"Blackie must have put them in there when he packed food for us."

"Remind me to thank Blackie if we ever see him again."

"Remind me to remind you to say thank you to him for this, too."

He held up a giant dildo. A two-inch wide mushroom-shaped head bulged from the nine-inch long base complete with fake veins. It was almost as big as Jarod's huge cock and it literally dripped with clear ointment. She knew instantly it was the special salve Jasmine had mentioned, the one that allowed a man to penetrate a virgin ass without her ever having to worry about being anally injured.

She blew out an aroused breath. "Blackie thinks of everything."

"That's what he was trained to do. Just as I."

He studied her for a moment longer before dropping to his knees beside her.

"Shall I explain a little of my sex slave training to you?"

She found herself swallowing at the excitement of his offer, and eagerly nodded wanting to know more about him and his years as a slave.

"The moment we males reach puberty, we are already fully trained in the art of being sex slaves, of being pleasure servants to women."

My God, they start the training so young.

"However up until then, we have not been allowed to touch a woman's supple flesh. We know all the erotic zones, where her every pleasure center is, but we have never touched a female's velvety skin. When we are finally allowed to touch…"

He reached out and trailed a line of fire as his fingers whispered down the valley of her heaving breasts. "When we are finally allowed to touch a women's flesh we are literally on fire. We are so eager to smooth our hands over her entire body, feeling the curves, exploring all her channels."

His finger gently pushed away her hand where she'd been playing with her nipple earlier, and tenderly ran a calloused fingertip over her hard bud.

"We are taught to be both gentle and rough with a woman's breasts. To pinch, to bite, to caress lightly and also how to outfit her with the vibrating clamps, if she likes."

"I like."

She could barely speak. Could barely breathe as he cupped her breast in his warm hand and squeezed. Dipping his head, his rough tongue brushed over her engorged nipple while his fingers squeezed her breast tenderly.

Soon his sharp teeth were nipping at her hardened bud until fire engulfed the stiff peak. Her pulse raced as he placed the nipple clamp onto her red bud and proceeded to cup her other breast.

His mouth and fingers worked wonders, and he had her other nipple hard and thick, and clamped within moments. The delicate gold chains felt cool against her fevered body as he arranged them over her belly and abdomen.

"You look so beautiful. So irresistible."

His breathing had grown even more labored. His eye had darkened to a lusty blue, and his full lips were ruby red from servicing her breasts.

"The most beautiful woman I have ever fucked. After you, there will be no other."

His sweet words overwhelmed her.

Here she was a kindergarten teacher from Earth, who'd almost given up on the idea of falling in love with a gentle, sexy man, and right now, this very instant, she knew deep in her heart she was in love with this handsome stranger, her knight in shining armor.

Who would have thought this was possible? That she would find herself a man millions of miles away from her home. On a godforsaken planet named Paradise where women ruled and men were nothing more than pleasure servants to females. And now she would have her very own sex slave.

"Tell me more about how you're trained?"

"I will show you. It will take many years to demonstrate to you all the different ways I can pleasure you, my heart."

His heart? How sweet. Those magical words sent shivers of affection humming through her.

From lowered lashes, she watched the strong tanned muscles in his lusciously curved ass ripple as he turned away from her and rained kisses down her belly and abdomen, then coming around her leg to nestle his body between her splayed legs.

"You have the most striking pink pussy, my heart. And your cream is gushing from you so quickly just as it had during your fever sex dreams."

He leaned over, and his hot breath cascaded against her pussy as he inhaled deeply.

"The scent of your sex is breathtaking. It is another reason why I could not allow Taylor to cure you with his mouth. For the cream might have intoxicated him into wanting you forever and I wished you to only be mine."

A frission of uneasiness zipped through her.

"What…what do you mean he'd want me forever?"

"It is said that the male or males who drink the infected female's arousal cream will be drawn to her for eternity."

"Oh." Disappointment like none she had ever felt gripped her.

His head snapped up at the sound of her voice.

"You do not seem pleased."

"I…I kind of thought…"

"What?"

"That you had genuine feelings for me. I didn't realize you were attracted to me because of…well that you were intoxicated or something."

Jarod growled with what she could only perceive as anger and suddenly dove between her legs. Her disappointment instantly dissolved as his tongue swiped erotically hard over her pulsing clitoris, making her belly clench with pleasure.

Back and forth, he swiped until a fierce heat burned there, and she was moaning beneath the onslaught.

"Does this feel as if I am doing it because some swamp water fever tells me to?"

Before she could answer, he sucked a plump pussy lip into his hot mouth and bit gently into her tender flesh. She jolted at the erotic sensations his tongue caused as it flicked against the pulsing delight caught between his sharp teeth.

He bit into her pussy lip until she burned and then he latched onto her other lip, nibbling erotically until her tiny piece of flesh was swollen and ablaze. Sucking sounds split the air, and when she let out a scream of arousal, he clamped her drenched pussy folds. In a flash, he also clamped her pulsing clitoris.

Sparks of pleasure-pain shot through each area he'd secured. A moment later the soft tinkling sound of chains drifted to her ears. She could feel the coolness of the decorative metal chains spray against her flesh, and suddenly all the clamps he'd placed on her body tingled to life, sending erotic vibrations scorching through her.

"Oh, sweet heavens!" she screamed, as her cunt and breasts throbbed with lusty pleasures.

"Does this make you believe the swamp water has grabbed my mind?"

She gasped as he turned up the vibrations. Perspiration blossomed over her fevered skin. His tongue dipped inside her pussy, and Piper cried out as a fantastic climax rolled over her. Without hesitation, she clasped her legs around his neck drawing his head closer until she was crushing his face against her quivering pussy.

Merciless explosions rattled her, twisted her.

She ground her hips against his face, gasped as his long tongue explored her very depths, sliding against her shattering pussy walls.

The carnal clamp sensations ebbed away and with them, her orgasms disintegrated.

She lay gasping in the tall grass; her arms splayed out at her sides, her swollen breasts heaving with her every aroused breath. Her nipples were red and hard, and oh so deliciously on fire. Her cunt ached and trembled as his tongue slid out of her vagina.

Firm masculine fingers lifted her trembling legs from around his neck, repositioning them as they'd been earlier, knees drawn up and feet wide apart.

"Do you still believe I am being controlled by the swamp water?" he rumbled, licking his lips.

His gaze raked across her face as he awaited an answer.

She tossed her head back and forth. "S-sorry. I b-believe you!"

"Don't ever doubt that you are my heart," he assured her gently, and suddenly she felt the lubricated tip of the dildo press against her anus.

"I won't." God! If making him upset brought her such fantastic orgasms, she'd have to do it more often.

"I was infatuated with you even before I tasted your pussy. You took my heart the instant I saw the innocence sparkling in your green eyes. Such sweet pure innocence toward a male I have never seen from a woman."

She swallowed hard at his lust-drenched voice.

"I shall continue with showing you more of my sex slave training."

He slid the dildo into her ass a little deeper, and at the same time rolled her tender clamped clit between his finger and thumb. Piper couldn't stop herself from whimpering at the delicious raw ache.

"Pain and pleasure are a delicate mix," Jarod whispered, as he watched her breathe through the pleasure-pain he inflicted. "You have to know just the right amount of combination in order to arouse a woman to sensual heights."

The dildo stopped momentarily.

He must have fiddled with the control box to the clamps because the metal that sweetly gripped her nipples suddenly vibrated to life again. Strong carnal sensations ripped through her breasts making her bite her bottom lip.

"You may massage your breasts if you like. Sometimes it counteracts the intensity of the pain."

She did as he instructed, massaging her now hard, swollen mounds in circular motions, feeling the quivering vibrations pummeling through the metal clamps as they rocked her glass-hard nipples.

She cried out as he dipped his head between her widespread legs again, and his rough tongue sliced up against her quivering clitoris and down to the crack of her ass. It tickled wonderfully. A moment later, he withdrew the dildo and his tongue nudged against her tight little hole, pressing hard until the sphincter of muscles gave way.

He slid inside.

She closed her eyes tightly and squirmed against him. His hot tongue tunneled and explored her anal canal sending blades of arousal shimmering wherever he touched. It felt so wonderful she thought she might have an orgasm on the spot, but he held her perched right on the delicate edge, his tongue throbbing as he dipped in and out in slow sensual movements, moving further and further inside.

She slid her ass back and forth across his face, loving the erotic scratching of his five o'clock shadow against the sensitive curve of her cheeks.

He withdrew his tongue and caressed the crack of her ass once again. Then the big, hard, lubricated dildo slid back in and drove easily the rest of the way deep into her ass, making her ass explode in blissful pleasure-pain that had her catching her breath.

Oh, sweet heavens!

The pain cleared quickly, replaced by a wild pleasurable feeling.

He began a slow erotic pumping of the lubed dildo. Thrusting into her ass until her hole was clenching and sucking at the smooth walls of the sex toy.

It felt so good, she reached up and played with her nipple clamps, pulling and tugging on them as she cried out at the blades of pleasure-pain spreading through her breasts and erupting deep inside her womb.

Her very empty womb that she needed filled up with Jarod's long, thick cock.

As if knowing what she needed, she felt his big solid piece of flesh kiss the entrance to her hot aching slit then he slid inside. She loved the way his cock stretched her muscles. Loved the way his hips slammed hard against hers and the way he pulsed and throbbed inside her vagina as he began a quick thrusting rhythm.

Big, strong thrusts that had his balls slapping against her flesh.

She squirmed against him eagerly accepting the fantastic stimulations of the pounding dildo and Jarod's cock.

Her body sparked and heaved with sensual pleasure, and she twisted and moaned beneath this wonderful onslaught of being double penetrated.

He fucked her hard.

Pounding the dildo into her ass.

Grinding his cock into her with all his strength.

Oh, yes! She'd wanted it rough and he was giving her his all.

Her pussy quivered. Spasmed. Her ass clenched. Burned.

The climax erupted from the fiery depths of her inflamed soul, snowballing, exploding through her like blades of lust.

His long, thick cock burned deeper into her vagina. She could feel him thicken inside her. Knew his release was near.

He thrust deeper, harder.

And exploded deep inside her, sending in hot jets of streaming sperm.

Her spasming depths milked him. Clutched desperately at his giant vein-riddled cock.

He pistoned harder.

Harder and harder, until she was screaming at the unbearable rapture, crying at the furious convulsions gripping her cum-flooded vagina.

Until she was sobbing at the kaleidoscope of carnal sensations enveloping her, and carrying her away into the erotic world of bliss.

* * * * *

"Missing? What do you mean they're missing, Piper?" her older brother Joe questioned her gently, and all three of her brothers peered through the soft glowing darkness at her, awaiting her answer.

Jarod had brought her here late this afternoon, and now Piper sat on a comfortable log in a small meadow flanked by her three brothers on one side of her and Jarod on the other. Finally clad in some proper attire, a long white T-shirt that her brothers had given her when they'd realized the sheet she'd come wrapped in was the only clothing she had, she couldn't help but notice the tense way Jarod kept looking at her since they'd arrived here. She wondered what was bothering him, but she would have to ask him later. Right now, she needed to explain to her brothers about their sisters.

Warm heat from the small friendly fire splashed against her bare legs. Overhead, Piper could make out those wildly dancing white lights in the night sky. They were the same ones she'd seen the night when Jarod had taken her up against that tree after she'd smelled the passion scented flower. Flushing with heat at the memory, she was grateful it was probably too dark for them to make out her blush.

When she'd arrived, she'd been enveloped in big bear hugs by her brothers, and quickly introduced to the women that they'd remained on the planet with. Joe's very pretty and very pregnant girlfriend Annie who was a Male Slave Doctor. Ben's girlfriend Jacey who Piper remembered as being a queen, along with their cute pudgy fifteen-month-old son Matthew. And finally, Buck's girlfriend Virgin and her two year old son Kiki, and their three fifteen-month-old adorable triplet daughters.

Now that the women and children had gone to their respective huts for the night, Piper had allowed herself to break down and start bawling while she'd broken the news about Kayla and Kinley.

"We crashed in the swamp. I remember fire and smoke, and water gushing in through a hole in the side of the spaceship. Kayla was screaming at me to pop the top hatch and to get out. I wanted to stay with her and help her with Kinley, but she just kept screaming at me to get out."

She couldn't stop the heated sobs from tearing out of her as she relayed more about the crash. "Kinley had been knocked unconscious at first. She woke up, and then there's this blank space that I can't remember. The next thing I know, all three of us were swimming together. You know what a lousy swimmer I am. I drank a lot of the swamp water, and then when we hit the shore I passed out. When I came to, I was in Jarod and Taylor's tree house."

She found herself growing hot when she remembered waking up to finding Jarod's face between her widespread legs hanging over his shoulders.

"We spotted their footsteps," Jarod continued for her. "Piper's twin, Kinley, appears to be covering her tracks. It could be because she had a run-in with the Death Valley Boys—"

Her brothers cursed heavily cutting him off, but Jarod quickly put up a hand to silence them. "She escaped unharmed. It is Kayla we are concerned for. Taylor is searching for her. I doubt the storms will stop him from finding her. We think she may have been taken by the Breeders."

Piper winced as all three of her brothers swore yet again.

"That's why we have to go back to the swamp and pick up their trail to search for them," Piper eagerly broke in, and brushed the hot tears from her cheeks.

Her brothers frowned and exchanged odd glances. They'd always looked that way when they were about to spring bad news.

Anxiety churned inside her. "What's the matter?"

"We can't go looking for them, at least not yet."

"Why not?"

"Because the stormy season is coming," Jarod answered for them. "With all the excitement, I had totally forgotten about the warning of the flickering white lights. The stormy season is upon us."

"So? A little bit of rain won't bother me. We can head out first thing in the morning."

"Piper," Ben broke in. "The storms here aren't like they're back in our time. They're bad, really bad. It'll rain and thunder for days. It isn't something to be caught out in. You know we would go out to look for them if there was a chance of finding them. But we have to wait until the storms are over."

Piper looked up at the flickering sky. The white lights seemed to be getting brighter. But she saw no sign of there being any storm clouds.

"There's no sign of lightning or anything. It's just harmless Northern Lights. And there hasn't been a drop of rain since I've been here."

"The storms come like clockwork. And we're due for the first one starting tonight," her brother Buck said.

Joe reached over and gave her a bear hug, holding her long and tight before letting her loose.

"I'm sorry, sis. But Kayla and Kinley are on their own for a little while longer. No matter how badly we want to go after them, we can't go out in it. We've experienced these storms, sweetie. We know the damage it can do. Going out there would compromise the safety of any rescue party. We need to stay safe until it passes and then we can go out and get them."

Piper nodded solemnly. The last thing she wanted to do was to put anyone's life at risk. She was new to this land. She had to trust her brothers and Jarod. Had to trust that they knew what was best for everyone.

"We should turn in before the storm hits," Joe said, and stood up. "You can tell us more about the spaceship crash tomorrow. But before we turn in, we need to know if we can safely return back to our time in Earth. Did our experiment work? Did the worms we placed into the sleep pods survive the year-long trip?"

"They made it just fine."

All her brothers smiled and cheered.

"But I don't understand. Why do you think there's a time warp?" she asked. "You didn't mention that in your coded messages."

Ben frowned. "Brace yourself for this, sis. But we found an exact duplicate of the Statue of Liberty on the shore of the nearby ocean. The Lady was old. Ancient. Virtually falling apart. We didn't know what to make of it. Didn't know if we'd gone through some time warp. So, we sent the worms back in time along with our coded messages. We figured if they made it back then we could take the women back with us."

Piper's heart leapt at the news. It meant there was a chance she could take Jarod back to Earth with her. He could be free of the death bounty on his head. Free of the wrath of Cath, and they'd be free to pursue their relationship.

"How bad was the spaceship after you left it?"

"Real bad. Like I said, it sunk."

"We can always salvage it," Ben said thoughtfully. "Especially if we get the replicator working again. If we have that, then we can duplicate the damaged parts."

"Sounds like a plan." Joe slapped her brothers on their backs, grinning like a Cheshire cat. "But first we'll go look for Kinley and Kayla after the storms let up."

"You can stay with Jacey and me and Matthew," Ben said to Piper as he stood and stretched his arms.

"And Jarod you can stay with Virgin and me and our kids. Virgin will want to catch up with you," Buck replied.

Jarod looked over at Piper. "I would prefer to stay in the guest house."

"So would I," Piper whispered, trying hard not to be embarrassed by her brothers' shocked looks.

"Oh! Sure, okay," Joe blubbered.

"Are you sure? I mean you barely know this guy and—" A quick poke to Buck's ribs from both his brothers made him shut up.

Jarod grabbed a hold of Piper's hand and pulled her off the log she'd been seated on.

"We're sure," she said, and followed him to what looked like a sod house nestled beneath a cliff in the darkness.

"See you when the storms are over," Jarod called to her three brothers who now stood beside the flickering fire with open-mouthed stares.

"Are you sure there isn't anything we can do to help my sisters?" Piper asked, as a few minutes later when Jarod led her into the cool interior of a small cozy eight-foot by eight-foot room built totally out of sod.

Shelves lined one of the walls. There were blankets and food, and utensils that she recognized as being from her brothers' spaceship. Obviously, they'd harvested lots of essentials before sending the spaceship back to Earth over two years ago.

"If we headed out now, we would only be bogged down in the storm. We would be useless, and I prefer not to be useless, at least not for the moment."

He took her into his arms and gazed into her eyes. Lust burned across his sexy five o'clock stubble-riddled face.

Gosh, the guy looked more and more dangerously sexy every day that went by.

"This is the sod house your brothers and their women stayed in on their first few nights in the valley. Are you sure you wish to stay here with me during the storms? They could last for days."

"Oh, I wish to stay all right." Piper reached up and curled her arms around his warm neck kissing him gently.

His lips were cool and moist as he tenderly kissed her back.

"And I wish for your cock to stay inside me all that time, too. Do you think you can handle that, big guy?"

Thunder rumbled in the distance and lightning flashed at the tiny oilcloth-covered windows.

"The storm is here," Jarod whispered.

"You can say that again." Piper smiled, fighting the torrents of passion searing through her as she cupped his sperm-heavy balls into the palms of her hands.

She trembled as his swollen erection pressed intimately against her pussy.

"Before we go any further, though, I want you to tell me why you've been looking so tense since we've gotten here."

"It is because of what you wear. I have not seen a woman wearing such a…sexy piece of clothing before. I've always been able to see through the material on a woman. This…" He pulled at the hem of the white T-shirt, and she felt the cool air slide against her fevered pussy as he lifted the material over her hips. "This piece of clothing leaves my imagination to go wild. It encourages me to find out what is beneath it. It lights a fire of curiosity inside me."

"This T-shirt turns you on?" Piper giggled, and lifted her arms allowing him to draw the top off her.

"It makes me want you so bad my cock burns to be locked inside of you."

He brushed his lips against hers, a tender kiss promising many wonderful things to come.

"You have me, Jarod. You have me for as long as you want me."

"I love you." His sweet words brought tears to her eyes.

He ground his hips against her, making her gasp at the thick erection poking against her mons.

"I want you forever, Piper Hero."

"Prove it," she whispered.

And he did.

Enjoy this excerpt from

A Hero Betrayed

© Copyright Jan Springer 2004

"Looks like we've caught ourselves a talking male."

"That's right honey. Now I'm ordering you to cut me down this minute or there will be hell to pay."

"There's a large bounty on the head of a talking male," another whispered, ignoring his command.

"Screw your bounty. I demand you to let me go."

"He must be one of those escaped educated sex slaves from last year's Slave Uprising."

Oh great! They thought he was a sex slave.

"Sex slaves are experts at pleasuring women," the cutest of the six said.

The women's blue gazes all brightened as they watched him curiously.

Uneasiness zipped up Buck's spine.

"Sorry ladies, but this guy ain't a sex slave. He's a free man, or at least I will be in a minute when you let me go."

"Quiet, slave, or it'll be the whip again!" the tall blonde snapped angrily.

Ookay, he could shut up. For a minute.

"We are not giving up this well-endowed male or the fun we've planned for ourselves just for a bounty!" The tall blonde addressed the others. Buck's hopes were dashed as all eagerly nodded in agreement.

The tall blonde spoke again, her harsh blue gaze clashed defiantly with Buck's. "And I, for one, do not want a male speaking while I fuck him. Perchance I should cut out his tongue?"

He didn't miss her hand slithering to the dagger strapped to her leg. Have mercy! These women were crazy!

"I have a better idea," another blonde chimed in. "We'll give him the passion poison now."

"The elders have warned 'tis dangerous to administer it without their guidance," one of them said quickly.

"But it will make him more obedient and quiet until they arrive," the tall blonde replied thoughtfully.

Oh man, he was screwed. Hopefully not literally.

"I'm up for a little danger." The woman who'd attacked his dick with an eager mouth grinned widely.

"I'm not interested!" Buck gasped as a whisper of panic threatened his sanity. "Cut me down. I've about had enough of this crap!"

The women's harsh intakes of breath made Buck tense. Obviously they didn't like being ordered around. The feminist movement was very much alive and well on this planet.

"The passion poison it is." The tall blonde smiled with smug satisfaction. From behind him he sensed movement. Before he could react, a sharp sting from a needle pierced the flesh of his right ass cheek.

He tried to swing himself away, but couldn't move more than a few inches.

He swore violently as the cool liquid flooded deep into his veins and spread an odd sensual heat throughout his tortured body.

The heat soothed the fiery whip welts, and languid weariness drifted through his limbs. He fought hard to keep his suddenly heavy eyelids from closing but knew he was quickly losing the battle.

"He's getting sleepy," the blonde who'd been sucking his cock giggled.

"It's too bad we'll have to kill him when we're through with him," someone else said. "His size would bring a fortune in the Brothel Town."

They were going to kill him? Oh boy, he'd really stepped into big-time trouble.

The whirring sound of the whip sliced through the air yet again and he gritted his teeth as savage pain snapped against his bare buttocks. This time however, the pain was brief, turning quickly into a savage erotic sensation that made Buck groan with want for more.

"It's working," a female uttered from somewhere nearby.

He shook his head to clear his fogging thoughts, but all that accomplished was giving one of the women free rein on his earlobe. She pressed a lusciously soft breast against his elbow as she nibbled on his flesh. Her warm silky hands slid wantonly over his sweaty chest until a hot ache throbbed throughout his body.

He found himself moaning at the wonderful sensations and to his horror he found himself craving more pleasure. His cock and balls grew painfully hard. He heard the women's sharp gasps and excited giggles.

"I've never seen a male so big!" one of them screamed.

"Take him down," another instructed in a rather hoarse voice. "Let's get him into the hide house. We'll get the Sacred Drink from him and then we'll let him rest. When he is fully adjusted to the passion poison, we're going to become women!"

Wild cheers pierced the warm evening air.

As they freed his limp legs, United States astronaut Buck Hero succumbed to the black tidal wave of sleep that swallowed him whole.

Enjoy this excerpt from
A Hero's Welcome
Heroes at Heart
© Copyright Jan Springer 2003

Chapter One

Sometime in the not so far future on a faraway planet…

Squeals of excitement rippling through the air prompted Annie Wilkes, Male Slave Doctor, to lift her head and see what was going on. She wasn't the least bit surprised to find five women trying to subdue a naked male slave in the hub square.

What did surprise her was the size of his penis. Unusually large, it bounced gallantly as he swiveled his bound legs up in an effort to kick at the women holding down his arms and head.

Annie had always fantasized about finding a male that big. A male she could dominate and use as her own personal sex toy. She licked her lips as lust rippled through her body.

The male struggled valiantly and she silently cheered him on. To her disappointment two of the women quickly grabbed the slave's legs and held him down on the ground.

Sweat beaded his muscular body. An ugly raw bullet wound marred the left side of his neck.

Annie forced her gaze away from the newly captured slave back to Cath, who stood stooped over beside her. Her mouth was warped in concentration as she tried to twist together the loose ends of a barbed wire fence that had rusted apart. Cath would know what was going on.

She was the slave catcher and trainer of their hub and owned all the incoming slaves.

"Cath, who is that male? I've never seen him before." She spoke casually. No use in letting Cath know she was interested in this male. It would only make her increase her price.

Cath's eyes narrowed as she followed Annie's gaze.

"That one's trouble. He's violent. Every woman in my crew has tried to mount him, but he won't let anyone do him."

"Where's he from? I don't see any markings."

"Found him in the Outer Limits. No brands. Most likely escaped the breeding camps when he was little. He's slated for castration. It'll make him more docile."

Annie bit her bottom lip in frustration.

"It seems such a waste. Males that big are rare."

"Might want to take a look at him after they're through with the castration. He got wounded when he was captured."

"Castration will prevent him from performing sexually for at least a few days." Annie pondered aloud.

Cath's head snapped up. "Do I detect a little interest in this slave?"

Annie's face suddenly flamed.

"My God! You want to fuck him, don't you?" Cath gasped.

Annie avoided Cath's amused smirk and looked over at the woman picking up the glowing castration knife from the crackling campfire.

Darn it. They were going to destroy him in a minute. She had to do something to stop them.

"Yes, I want to fuck him. Do me a favor. Don't castrate him. Not yet."

"I don't do favors, Annie. I'll want something in return."

Annie watched wide-eyed with frustration as the knife-wielding woman hunkered down over the struggling male. Impatience soared through her.

"Name your price later. I'll do whatever you want."

"He won't be a willing participant."

Annie forced herself to focus her attention back to Cath and winked. "They make the best kind."

About the author:

Jan Springer is the pseudonym for an award winning best selling author who writes erotic romance and romantic suspense at a secluded cabin nestled in the Haliburton Highlands, Ontario, Canada.

She has enjoyed careers in hairstyling and accounting, but her first love is always writing. Hobbies include kayaking, gardening, hiking, traveling, reading and writing.

Jan welcomes mail from readers. You can write to her c/o Ellora's Cave Publishing at 1056 Home Avenue, Akron, OH 44310-3502.

Why an electronic book?

We live in the Information Age—an exciting time in the history of human civilization in which technology rules supreme and continues to progress in leaps and bounds every minute of every hour of every day. For a multitude of reasons, more and more avid literary fans are opting to purchase e-books instead of paperbacks. The question to those not yet initiated to the world of electronic reading is simply: *why?*

1. *Price.* An electronic title at Ellora's Cave Publishing and Cerridwen Press runs anywhere from 40-75% less than the cover price of the <u>exact same title</u> in paperback format. Why? Cold mathematics. It is less expensive to publish an e-book than it is to publish a paperback, so the savings are passed along to the consumer.

2. *Space.* Running out of room to house your paperback books? That is one worry you will never have with electronic novels. For a low one-time cost, you can purchase a handheld computer designed specifically for e-reading purposes. Many e-readers are larger than the average handheld, giving you plenty of screen room. Better yet, hundreds of titles can be stored within your new library—a single microchip. (Please note that Ellora's Cave and Cerridwen Press does not endorse any specific brands. You can check our website at www.ellorascave.com or

www.cerridwenpress.com   for   customer
recommendations   we   make   available   to   new
consumers.)

3. *Mobility.* Because your new library now consists of
   only a microchip, your entire cache of books can be
   taken with you wherever you go.

4. *Personal preferences are accounted for.* Are the words you
   are   currently   reading   too   small?   Too   large?
   Too...**ANNOYING**? Paperback books cannot be
   modified according to personal preferences, but e-
   books can.

5. *Instant gratification.* Is it the middle of the night and all
   the bookstores are closed? Are you tired of waiting
   days — sometimes   weeks — for   online   and   offline
   bookstores to ship the novels you bought? Ellora's
   Cave Publishing sells instantaneous downloads 24
   hours a day, 7 days a week, 365 days a year. Our e-
   book delivery system is 100% automated, meaning
   your order is filled as soon as you pay for it.

   Those are a few of the top reasons why electronic
novels are displacing paperbacks for many an avid reader.
As always, Ellora's Cave and Cerridwen Press welcomes
your questions and comments. We invite you to email us
at service@ellorascave.com, service@cerridwenpress.com
or write to us directly at: 1056 Home Ave. Akron OH
44310-3502.

The
ELLORA'S CAVE
Library

Stay up to date with Ellora's Cave Titles
in Print with our Quarterly Catalog.

To recieve a catalog,
send an email with your name
and mailing address to:

CATALOG@ELLORASCAVE.COM

or send a letter or postcard
with your mailing address to:
Catalog Request
c/o Ellora's Cave Publishing, Inc.
1337 Commerce Drive #13
Stow, OH 44224

Lady Jaided magazine is devoted to exploring the sexuality and sensuality of women. While there are many similarities between the sexual experiences of men and women, there are just as many if not more differences. Our focus is on the female experience and on giving voice and credence to it. Lady Jaided will include everything from trends, politics, science and history to gossip, humor and celebrity interviews, but our focus will remain on female sexuality and sensuality.

A Sneak Peek at Upcoming Stories

Clan of the Cave Woman
Women's sexuality throughout history.

The Sarandon Syndrome
What's behind the attraction between older women and younger men.

The Last Taboo
Why some women – even feminists – have bondage fantasies

Girls' Eyes for Queer Guys
An in-depth look at the attraction between straight women and gay men

Available Spring 2005

Lady Jaided Regular Features

Jaid's Tirade
Jaid Black's erotic romance novels sell throughout the world, and her publishing company Ellora's Cave is one of the largest and most successful e-book publishers in the world. What is less well known about Jaid Black, a.k.a. Tina Engler is her long record as a political activist. Whether she's discussing sex or politics (or both), expect to see her get up on her soapbox and do what she does best: offend the greedy, the holier-than-thous, and the apathetic! Don't miss out on her monthly column.

Devilish Dot's G-Spot
Married to the same man for 20 years, Dorothy Araiza still basks in a sex life to be envied. What Dot loves just as much as achieving the Big O is helping other women realize their full sexual potential. Dot gives talks and advice on everything from which sex toys to buy (or not to buy) to which positions give you the best climax.

On the Road with Lady K
Publisher, author, world traveler and Lady of Barrow, Kathryn Falk shares insider information on the most romantic places in the world.

Kandidly Kay
This Lois Lane cum Dave Barry is a domestic goddess by day and a hard-hitting sexual deviancy reporter by night. Adored for her stunning wit and knack for delivering one-liners, this Rodney Dangerfield of reporting will leave no stone unturned in her search for the bizarre truth.

A Model World
CJ Hollenbach returns to his roots. The blond heartthrob from Ohio has twice been seen in Playgirl magazine and countless other publications. He has appeared on several national TV shows including The Jerry Springer Show (God help him!) and has been interviewed for Entertainment Tonight, CNN and The Today Show. He has been involved in the romance industry for the past 12 years, appearing on dozens of romance novel covers and calendars. CJ's specialty is personal interviews, in which people have a tendency to tell him everything.

Hot Mama Cooks
Sex is her food, and food is her sex. Hot Mama gives aphrodisiac a whole new meaning. Join her every month for her latest sensual adventure -- with bonus recipe!

Empress on the Mount
Brash, outrageous, and undeniably irreverent, this advice columnist from down under will either leave you in stitches or recovering from hang-jaw as you gawk at her answers to reader questions on relationships and life.

Erotic Fiction from Ellora's Cave
The debut issue will feature part one of "Ferocious," a three-part erotic serial written especially for Lady Jaided by the popular Sherri L. King.

Printed in the United States
30742LVS00001B/112-147